BY JOHN FEINSTEIN

THE SPORTS BEAT SERIES

Last Shot: Mystery at the Final Four

Vanishing Act: Mystery at the U.S. Open

Cover-Up: Mystery at the Super Bowl

Change-Up: Mystery at the World Series

The Rivalry: Mystery at the Army-Navy Game

Rush for the Gold: Mystery at the Olympics

THE TRIPLE THREAT SERIES

The Walk On

The Sixth Man

The DH

Foul Trouble

Backfield Boys

The Prodigy

THE BENCHWARMERS SERIES

Benchwarmers

Game Changers

Mixed Doubles

MIXED DOUBLES

JOHN FEINSTEIN

FARRAR STRAUS GIROUX · NEW YORK

Farrar Straus Giroux Books for Young Readers
An imprint of Macmillan Publishing Group, LLC
120 Broadway, New York, NY 10271

mackids.com

Our books may be purchased in bulk for promotional, educational, or business use. Please contact your local bookseller or the Macmillan Corporate and Premium Sales Department at (800) 221-7945, ext. 5442, or by email at MacmillanSpecialMarkets@macmillan.com.

Library of Congress Cataloging-in-Publication Data

Names: Feinstein, John, author.
Title: Mixed doubles / John Feinstein.
Description: First edition. | New York : Farrar Straus Giroux Books for Young Readers, 2022. | Series: Benchwarmers ; 3 | Audience: Grades 4–6. | Summary: Eleven-year-old Andi Carillo quickly becomes the star of her school's new co-ed tennis team, and when her talent attracts sports agents who want her to play professionally, Andi's best friend Jeff Michaels helps her thwart the agents by uncovering their underhanded schemes.
Identifiers: LCCN 2021027781 | ISBN 9780374312077 (hardcover)
Subjects: CYAC: Tennis—Fiction. | Sports agents—Fiction. | Ability—Fiction. | Middle schools—Fiction. | Schools—Fiction. | Philadelphia (Pa.)—Fiction. | LCGFT: Novels. | Sports fiction.
Classification: LCC PZ7.F3343 Mi 2022 | DDC [Fic]—dc23
LC record available at https://lccn.loc.gov/2021027781

First edition, 2022
Book design by Trisha Previte

Printed in the United States of America by LSC Communications, Harrisonburg, Virginia
ISBN: 978-0-374-31207-7
1   3   5   7   9   10   8   6   4   2

This is for Mary Carillo, who somehow still loves tennis every single day in spite of the sport's flaws.

1

JEFF MICHAELS THOUGHT HE WAS GOING TO GET TO THE ball—except that he had miscalculated how hard it had been hit. He lunged for it, racquet extended as far as possible, and then watched helplessly as it whizzed past him and bounced off the back wall of the court.

"Nice shot," he said for what felt like the thousandth time that morning. Andi Carillo just smiled, walked to the baseline, and got into her service-returning stance.

Jeff picked up the ball she had just blasted past him and a second one that was lying behind the court and walked to the baseline to serve.

"Thirty–forty," he said. His parents had taught him it was always the server's job to call out the score so there would be no confusion about it.

There was little confusion about how badly Andi

was beating Jeff. It was a clear, cool late March day in Philadelphia, and they were playing on a public court not far from Jeff's house. It had been Andi's idea to get out and play before tryouts for the Merion Middle School tennis team began on Monday. When she'd thrown in the fact that they could go to their favorite pizza place for lunch afterward—courtesy of a ride from her father—he'd jumped at the idea.

Now he wished he'd called in sick.

It was no surprise that Andi was a good tennis player. They had talked throughout the winter about how much they enjoyed playing, and Jeff already knew from soccer and basketball seasons that Andi was a very good athlete.

But *this* good he hadn't been ready for. He could tell, even when they were warming up, that Andi had that feel for the game that only excellent players have. Jeff thought he was pretty good for someone who wouldn't be twelve until the summer, and he'd done well in some age-group tournaments the previous couple of years. But Andi was very clearly on a different level.

It wasn't about power. When Jeff had lost in tournaments, it was usually to kids who were bigger and stronger than he was and overpowered him. Jeff had grown during the school year and was now five foot six and 140 pounds and in shape, having played both soccer and basketball.

Andi was still a little taller than he was and weighed a good deal less. But she was almost blindingly fast, and her two-handed backhand rocketed off her racquet with as much speed as her whipsaw forehand. Jeff was a pretty good tennis player. Andi, he reasoned, was more of a prodigy.

"Set point, right?" she called back after his announcement of the score.

Jeff had almost forgotten. The two sets they'd played had gone so fast it was, in fact, already set point. She'd won the first set 6–1, and it was now 3–5 with Jeff serving in the second. Jeff had played better in the second set after adapting to the fact that just about anything he hit was coming back, even when he thought he'd hit a winner. The closest thing Andi had to an Achilles' heel was her serve. It wasn't bad, it just didn't have the power of her forehand or her backhand. This wasn't uncommon in kids their age. Jeff's serve didn't exactly remind anyone of Roger Federer.

"Yeah, set point," he said, almost relieved the match was almost over. They had agreed to play best-of-three. There would be no need, he thought, to play three.

His first serve, which he attempted to crush, sailed way long. He saw Andi creeping inside the baseline waiting to blast his weak second serve. He tried to spin it to her backhand—and succeeded. But it didn't matter. She took one step to her left, lined up the looping ball, and slammed it into the corner, the ball landing inches inside the baseline and the sideline. Jeff didn't bother to move.

"Nice," he said for what felt like the millionth time of the morning.

She smiled, pulled her cap off, and let her long brown hair down from the bun she'd stuffed up into her cap in order to play.

They met at the net and formally shook hands like real tennis players.

"Why didn't you tell me you're so good?" he said as they walked off the court, picked up water bottles, and sat down, side-by-side.

"How good I am never came up, did it?" she said with a smile. "We just agreed it would be good to get out and play before the tryouts started, right?"

She was—as usual—right.

The middle school district in which Merion was located had announced two weeks earlier that, going forward, tennis teams would be co-ed. Andi was, at the very least, partly responsible for this.

When Merion had formed a sixth grade soccer team the previous fall, she wanted to be part of it even though the team was supposed to be for boys, since the girls had a field hockey team. Even though the soccer coach had done everything possible to keep her off the team and then—having been forced to allow her onto the team by the school principal—had kept her nailed to the bench, she had ended up starring for the Mustangs.

With tennis a new sport at the middle school level that spring, the decision had been made to make the teams co-ed. There would be three girls' singles matches and three boys' singles matches when teams played one another. There would also be one boys' doubles match, one girls' doubles match and, if the teams were tied at 4–4, a mixed doubles match would decide the outcome.

Players could only play a second match if the mixed doubles were needed to break a tie. Jeff was certain that Andi would be Merion's number one singles player on the girls' side and would play mixed doubles whenever it had to be played.

He was a lot less certain about how he'd fit in or *if* he'd fit in. Unlike in soccer and basketball, this was not just a sixth grade team. He'd be competing with seventh and eighth graders. Andi would, too, but he was confident she could handle the older kids. He wasn't nearly as confident about how he would do when the tryouts began.

He took a long sip of water and asked Andi if she was ranked in the East. He knew tennis had rankings starting with ten-and-unders both regionally and nationally.

She gave him a funny look and then said, "Well, yeah, I was ranked third in the East last year."

Jeff almost gasped, but held it in. One thing he knew about age-group tennis was that most players didn't get into the top ten or maybe even the top twenty until they were at the top of the age group—especially the younger ones where kids were still growing.

Andi wouldn't be twelve until May. That meant as an eleven-year-old the previous summer—a newly turned eleven-year-old—she'd only had two players ranked ahead of her in the eastern zone of the country.

"I'm guessing there weren't a lot of eleven-year-olds in the top ten," he said.

She sipped her water as if she hadn't heard him and stood up to head off the court.

"Let me guess," he said, standing to follow her out. "You were the only one."

"True," she said finally.

"What about nationally?" he asked.

"I was tenth," she answered.

"Any other eleven-year-olds in the top ten?" he asked.

"No," she said. "Let's go get some pizza."

2

IT HAD BECOME SOMETHING OF A SATURDAY TRADITION
during the basketball season for Jeff and Andi to go
to Andy's Pizza at the King of Prussia Mall and then
wander the mall or go to a movie.

Andi really liked Jeff. He had played an important role in getting her on the soccer team in the fall
by getting his father—who worked at NBC Sports–
Philadelphia—to publicize the coach's refusal to put a
girl on his team even though she had clearly been one
of the best players during tryouts.

Now the two of them talked daily, either in person
at school or over text or occasionally on the phone.
Some days it was all three.

Andi knew Jeff had a crush on her. She liked him
as a friend—a lot—and thought there might come a
time when they might be more than friends. But not

now; not before they turned twelve and were still in the sixth grade.

And not while she was caught up in sports. She loved soccer and basketball and was good at both, but there was no doubt the sport where she excelled was tennis. She also knew that any letdown in her grades would mean she wouldn't get to play *any* sport. Both her parents were lawyers. She had a brother at Penn and another one at Columbia. One *B* on a report card might be excused. Not two.

It wasn't as if her parents didn't enjoy sports. Both her brothers were athletes, but Andi was the real jock in the family. It helped that both her parents *loved* tennis and had introduced her to it at a young age. By the time she was six, she was hitting regularly with her two older brothers. The fact that there were six public courts within walking distance of the house helped a lot.

She'd taken lessons at Blue Bell Racquet Club from the pro there, Dennis DeStefano, and she was competing in ten-and-under events by the time she was eight. DeStefano had encouraged her parents to make tennis a twelve-month-a-year sport for her, and he even brought up the notion of sending her to a sports academy so she could focus all year round on her tennis.

Thankfully, her parents had emphatically rejected the idea and had limited tennis to being a spring and summer sport for her. She knew that many of the kids she was competing with played *just* tennis and there were occasions—usually after a loss to one of them— that she wondered how much better she would be if she focused only on tennis.

But she loved team sports, even if playing on the soccer and basketball teams during her sixth grade year had been full of rocky moments. And she knew her parents were right when they said that the number of athletes who burned out on a sport playing it all the time was a lot bigger than the number who became stars.

After her mother had dropped her and Jeff at the mall, they ordered their traditional six-slice pizza. Jeff usually would eat four slices, Andi two, although there were times when she called dibs on a third. Andi was fairly certain that Jeff could eat the entire pizza given the chance. He was slender, not an ounce of fat on him, but he could inhale food—especially pizza—as fast as anyone Andi had ever seen. Even faster than her older brothers, who had a tendency to finish their dinners before anyone else in the family had taken two bites.

"You sure we shouldn't get the large pie with eight slices?" she said as they stepped up to order.

"I'm sure," he said.

"Why not?" she said.

"Because if we get eight slices, I'll eat six and you'll

eat two and I'll spend the rest of the day feeling like there's a rock sitting in my stomach."

Once they'd found empty seats—not easy on a spring Saturday—Jeff began doing his "Jeff" thing—interrogating her in great detail about her tennis experiences.

She understood. Jeff's dad had worked at NBC Sports–Philly for about ten years but had been a newspaper reporter for almost two decades before that. Jeff had reporting in his genes. That meant asking a lot of questions. Unfortunately, he'd played enough tennis and followed junior tennis enough that he knew what questions to ask.

"Have you played in the Orange Bowl?" he asked, referencing the most important tournament for kids fourteen-and-under.

She shook her head. "My parents didn't want me to go this year because it's over Christmas break. I might go next year."

There were lots more: Best player she'd faced? Best player she'd beaten? Did she want to be a pro someday?

Finally, she stopped him by changing the subject to Merion Middle's tennis-team-to-be.

"Maybe we'll get to play mixed doubles together," she said. "That would be fun, huh?"

He laughed. "I don't even know if I'll make the team," he said. "Remember, this isn't just sixth grade—it's the entire school. Who knows how many good players there will be at tryouts?"

"You'll make the team," she said. "You're a good player."

"You just dusted me one-and-three and you weren't even breathing hard," he said, raising his voice.

"Yeah well, there's just one thing about that," she said.

"What?" he asked.

"I'm really good," she answered.

They both laughed and Jeff grabbed another slice of pizza.

3

JEFF WASN'T SURE HOW TO FEEL ON MONDAY AFTERNOON when he walked onto Merion Middle's four tennis courts—all hard courts, no doubt because they were far easier to maintain than clay courts—for the first day of tennis team tryouts.

Merion was one of three middle schools in the Philadelphia district that had tennis courts. Different schools had different "bonus" facilities. Four schools had swimming pools; one had an ice rink. Jeff was glad Merion had tennis courts, especially since his swimming and ice-skating skills were minimal.

Although he wasn't surprised, it felt funny to look around and see no one who had been on either the sixth grade soccer team or the boys' sixth grade basketball team—other than Andi.

There were ten boys and twelve girls dressed in

various forms of tennis clothes—no one in what was once considered the traditional all-white. As far as Jeff knew, the only place left in the world where all-white outfits were still required was Wimbledon.

It was a cool afternoon and Jeff was wearing a maroon Temple basketball sweatshirt and sweatpants. Andi, he noticed, was also wearing sweats. Her sweatshirt said COLUMBIA SOCCER. There were two coaches—neither of whom Jeff knew. Both were eighth grade teachers: Bill Foster taught algebra and Joan O'Grady taught history. They introduced themselves as co-coaches and quickly pointed out that neither was there to exclusively coach boys or girls.

"We're both here to help you kids improve and to work together as a team, which is important, even though people think of tennis as an individual sport," Coach Foster said. "Our first job, though, is going to be to pick a team, which I'm sure won't be easy."

"We've got spots for five boys and five girls," said Coach O'Grady. "The format for our dual matches calls for six singles matches—three boys' and three girls': two doubles—one boys', one girls'—and, if need be, a mixed doubles match. Everyone will play in either a singles or a doubles match. Then, if we need to play mixed, Coach Foster and I will decide who plays."

The fact that a team needed five players for each

match was, Jeff decided, a good thing. He still had no idea how good anyone else who had shown up was—except for Andi—so five guaranteed spots for boys and five for girls increased his chances of surviving the cut.

"We're going to pick the team very objectively," Coach Foster said. "Everyone is going to play one eight-game pro set against one another over the next three days. We'll add up won-lost records, and the top five boys and the top five girls will make the team."

"What if there's a tie?" one of the girls asked. Jeff realized he *did* know her. It was Lisa Carmichael, who had been on the sixth grade girls' basketball team and was one of Andi's close friends. She'd gotten a short haircut and looked completely different, which is why he hadn't recognized her at first.

"We'll tiebreak based on number of games won," Coach O'Grady answered. "If a match gets to 7–all, we'll play a tiebreak so no one has the advantage of serving in the last game. Keep in mind that total games won might be a tiebreaker and try to win every game you possibly can. It could matter."

"We've only got room for sixteen players to warm-up at a time, four to a court," Coach Foster added, "so we'll do it alphabetically. Everyone gets ten minutes, then we'll start playing. Match assignments will start alphabetically, too."

Jeff was assigned to warm up with Melanie Nuzzo,

who he actually knew from his English class. She was left-handed, which was a little bit distracting as they got started, but he adapted quickly. His guess was that unless there wasn't much depth on the girls' side, Melanie wasn't likely to make the team.

Tennis was funny that way: You could almost always tell a player from a non-player in a few swings of the racquet.

After they'd been hitting for a while, Coach Foster blew a whistle and said, "Everyone hit some serves."

They did as instructed, and then the last six players took the court. Two courts were open. "Take a water break and then let's get the first matches started," Coach O'Grady said.

One boys' match and one girls' match started soon after. Jeff didn't know enough names to guess who he'd play first. When the last two courts were opened up, Andi was sent out to play Lisa Carmichael. That made sense since both their last names began with *C*.

Lisa Carmichael was a good player, so good that she actually won three games from Andi and took a couple of other games to deuce. By the time they finished, everyone not playing at that moment was watching them.

"If they're not the two best girls we have, I'd like to see who is," Tommy Arnold said to Jeff. Arnold had been a manager for the boys' basketball team, and he was clearly a good tennis player. He had won the first boys' match and was sitting on the same bench where Jeff was waiting to be called.

"If there's a girl better than Andi, then we should be playing against Villanova or Penn, not King of Prussia Middle," Jeff said.

Arnold smiled. "You're just saying that because you're in love with her."

Jeff was now accustomed to being teased about how he felt about Andi. "You really think that's it?" he said in response.

Arnold shook his head. "No, I don't," he said. "Not even close."

Before everyone was sent home at six o'clock, three rounds had been completed. Jeff was feeling very good about himself. He had gone 3–0, winning one match 8–0 against Alan Scheer, who clearly was out of his element. His last match, against Art Schnabel, had gone to the 7–all tiebreak. At 5–5, Schnabel had choked—first serving a double fault and then netting what should have been a sitter forehand, trying to do too much with the shot, giving Jeff the game, 7–5, and the match, 8–7.

Jeff knew he'd been a little bit lucky but wasn't complaining. He knew he was one of three boys who had gone 3–0 on the day. There were six more matches to play over the next two days, but it was a good start.

Andi didn't lose another game in her last two matches. Not surprisingly, Lisa Carmichael won her next two matches easily. The only other girl to go 3–0 was Mindy Garceau, who was about six-feet tall and had a serve that seemed to come from just under the clouds.

"So, when do you play her?" Jeff asked Andi as they walked toward the locker rooms when the session was over.

"I guess tomorrow," Andi said. "I don't think she'll be a problem. There's not that much to her game beyond her serve."

"The serve's pretty good though, no?" Jeff said.

"It's very good," Andi said. "But there's more to tennis than a good serve. Look at John Isner."

Jeff knew the name but not much more. Andi could tell.

"He's six-ten—about her height," she joked with a smile. "Almost unbreakable serve. Good player. Made the Wimbledon semis once. But he's never won anything that matters because he can't *break* serve."

"He must break it some of the time to win matches."

"Not so much," she said. "He wins a lot of tiebreaks."

She changed the subject. "I didn't get to watch you that much, but 3–0 should make you feel pretty comfortable."

"Lot of tennis left to go," he said.

"What're you, a football coach?" she said. "You going to step up and give 110 percent tomorrow?"

They both liked to joke about jock-clichés. Because of his father's job, Jeff had heard them all.

"Yeah," he said. "And then I'll give all the glory to God."

"And to your teammates," Andi said as they turned to head to their separate locker rooms.

"A-men," Jeff said. "A-men."

4

WHEN THE TRYOUTS WERE OVER, ANDI HAD FINISHED 9–0.
Two of the girls had thrown in the proverbial towel
after the second day with 0–6 match records. One, as
Jeff had predicted before the end of the first day, was
Melanie Nuzzo.

Lisa Carmichael was second at 8–1, her only loss
being to Andi. Mindy Garceau was third at 7–2, her
only losses being to Andi and Lisa. Andi had beaten
her 8–1 and had been a little annoyed with herself
for giving up the game she had lost. Then again, she
had never touched a ball in the game Garceau had
won: She'd served four aces and two double faults. At
40–30, she'd hit a serve right down the middle that
Andi thought might be an inch or two wide, but she'd
called it good because her parents had always taught

her that if an opponent hit a shot that *might* be good, you called it good.

That wasn't always the case with some of her opponents in age-group matches, but Andi had always played it that way.

When Andi served out the match in the next game and they shook hands at the net, Garceau, who had moved to Philadelphia from France the previous year and spoke perfect English with a barely noticeable accent, said to her: "Are you sure my last serve wasn't wide?"

Andi shrugged. "Thought it was perfect," she said. "Right on the line."

Garceau smiled and said, "You are as good a person as you are a player."

Andi felt as if she'd made a new friend. In fact, Andi was thrilled when the coaches announced the final standings for the girls: Andi, Lisa Carmichael, Garceau, Jane Blythe—the only lefty in the group—and Patricia Gerson. Patty had won the last spot over Hillary James because she'd won a total of forty-seven games to Hillary's forty-four.

That was a tough way to miss out on making the team, but the coaches had been clear about the tiebreaker from the start.

Andi liked all four girls who had made the team with her. Outside of Jeff, she didn't know the boys as well, but they all seemed like nice guys. This was very different than soccer, where a number of the boys had resented her presence at tryouts and then on the team, and basketball, where the team had been divided into cliques for the first half of the season, largely because of a coach who was both inexperienced and a latent racist.

This was a relief. This should be fun.

There was no need for any tiebreakers among the boys. The top five clearly separated themselves from the bottom four. Jeff and Gary Morrissey finished tied for first at 7–1; Jeff earning the No. 1 spot because he'd beaten Gary head-to-head. His only loss was in a tiebreak to Tommy Arnold, who finished third at 6–2. Art Schnabel and Jose Aguilar finished tied for fourth at 5–3. The other guys had losing records.

The coaches thanked everyone who had gone through all three days and the players who had been cut headed inside. Then, they explained the schedule to the ten players on the team. They would practice Thursday and Friday. For the moment, the fourth and fifth qualifiers would be the doubles team on each side. On Monday, they would give the players some time to play mixed doubles to see who might work together best.

The season would begin the following Tuesday against Main Line. Only seven schools in the district had teams, so they would play a dozen matches—two against each school. The schools that didn't have their own courts had access to courts that they would use for their home matches.

"Andi and anybody," was Arnold's assessment of who should play mixed doubles after the coaches had told them all to go and shower.

Schnabel, walking beside them, nodded. "We're starting every match up 1–0. No one's going to beat her."

Jeff wasn't thinking they were wrong.

"How'd she do against our thirteen and fourteen year olds?" said Schnabel, who was a seventh grader. "She dusted all the girls and probably would dust all of us."

Jeff didn't argue that point. He'd finished tied for first with Morrissey—an eighth grader—among the boys and had played two matches that had gone to tie-break games. None of the boys had been clearly better than he was. Andi *was* clearly better than he was.

"There are maybe some older boys in the district who are better than she is," Schnabel continued. "Size and strength become factors when you're a teenager. But girls? I don't see it. Unless there's a budding Coco Gauff at one of the schools."

"If there was one, she'd probably already be shipped off to a tennis academy somewhere," Arnold said.

Gauff had become a sensation in the summer of 2019 when, at the age of fifteen, she'd upset Venus Williams at Wimbledon and reached the round of sixteen.

"Actually," Schnabel said, "I'm a little surprised Andi's parents haven't thought about sending her to one of those places. A lot of kids who go there end up making a lot of money. I mean, she's that good."

"Doesn't matter," Jeff said confidently. "Her parents like it that Andi's a good athlete, but they aren't going to get caught up in the one sport for twelve-months-a-year thing that so many parents fall for. They'd rather she be happy than rich."

"I'd rather be both," Arnold said.

"Me too," Schnabel said.

They all laughed. Like Andi, Jeff found himself enjoying the start of tennis season a lot more than he'd enjoyed the beginnings of soccer and basketball season.

What's more, Schnabel was probably right: Merion would almost certainly start most matches up 1–0, courtesy of his friend Andi Carillo.

5

AS IT TURNED OUT, ANDI'S 6–1, 6–2 WIN OVER MAIN LINE'S number one female singles player was just the start of an easy opening victory for Merion on Tuesday afternoon.

Jeff won his match almost as convincingly—6–3, 6–2—and the only match Main Line won was the boys' doubles. It was easy to understand why Art Schnabel and Jose Aguilar lost interest after splitting the first two sets. Merion was up 7–0 and, while a shutout would have been nice, it was getting close to dinnertime and everyone wanted to go home. Schnabel lost serve at 4–all in the last set and the two Main Line kids celebrated their win as if it had decided the day's outcome.

Aguilar was muttering something coming off the court about "scoreboard." As in, the final score of the overall match was 7–1. They did their cheers, and Jeff and Andi went to greet Jeff's mom, who was picking them both up.

Andi's parents were both stuck working—her dad, who was a litigator, had been in court all afternoon—and Jeff's dad had a Flyers game to cover that night. That left Arlene Michaels with the pickup duty.

"Nice going, you two," she said as her son and his friend approached. "You guys made that look easy."

"How much did you see?" Jeff asked, not sure when his mom had arrived.

"I saw all of your second set and"—looking at Andi—"the last couple games of your match. You didn't need very much time out there, did you?"

Andi was about to answer when a man in a blue pinstriped suit approached. He was young—no more than thirty, Jeff guessed—and extremely overdressed for a junior high school tennis match on a Tuesday afternoon in late March.

"Excuse me," he said, looking first at Andi and then at Jeff's mom. "Don't mean to interrupt, but just wanted to introduce myself to you, Andrea, and to your mom."

Jeff instantly disliked him, in part because he'd ignored him completely, but also because he had said he didn't mean to interrupt when he was clearly interrupting.

"If you want to talk to my mom, you'll need to call her law office," Andi said, clearly as put off as Jeff as she reluctantly shook the guy's hand.

"Oh, really sorry, I just assumed . . ."

"Yes, you did," Jeff's mom said. "I'm Arlene Michaels and this is my son, Jeff. What can we do for you?"

Jeff almost laughed. The guy had clearly gone three-for-three when it came to getting off to a bad start.

"Oh, of course, sorry," the guy said, reddening just a little.

A business card suddenly appeared in his right hand. Maybe he's a magician, Jeff thought.

Not so much.

"My name's Tad Walters," he said. "Just wanted to say hi and congratulate you on how you played today, Andrea. I work for a group called ProStyles and we represent athletes all over the world . . ."

"You're an agent?" Jeff's mom said, clearly a little stunned and a little angry. "What in the world could you possible want with an eleven-year-old girl?"

Walters smiled, clearly not bothered by the question.

"Mrs. Murphy . . ."

"Michaels," Jeff's mom said. "It's Michaels."

"Sorry," he said. "Of course, Andrea doesn't need an agent now. But with her talent, there's going to come a day—"

"And when that day comes, if it ever comes, my parents will represent me," Andi said. "They're both lawyers. I won't need an agent then and I certainly don't need one now."

Walters still had the card hanging from his fingertips. "Well, it can't hurt to do some homework, can it?"

He pushed the card in Andi's direction. She was turning her back on him. Jeff grabbed the card. "I'll hold it for her," he said.

Walters stared at him, clearly unsure what to say or do. Finally, he smiled. "Great," he said. "Never hurts to have the boyfriend on your side."

"We're teammates. And friends," Jeff said quickly, even as Andi started to turn back around. He smiled what he hoped was a phony-looking smile. "But I'm happy to take care of the card for you."

"Thanks," Walters said, shaking Jeff's hand.

"Oh, you're welcome," Jeff said. "You're very welcome."

"What was that about?" Andi asked, glaring at Jeff when Walters finally walked away. "Why in the world would you take his card?"

Jeff grinned. "I think my dad would find it fascinating that an agent is trying to talk to an eleven-year-old, don't you?"

Andi groaned. "No, not again," she said. "I do *not* need any more publicity."

"But this is different," Jeff said. "You aren't fighting to get on a team or even with an incompetent coach. You're just a really good tennis player."

They were getting in the car now. Jeff sat in back next to his friend.

"I don't care," she said. "All I want is one season where I can just play and not have people coming up to me and saying they saw me on TV or—worse—that I'm some kind of publicity hound."

Jeff's dad and his TV station had played a big role in getting Andi onto the soccer team in the fall after she'd been cut for committing the crime of being a girl. His station, NBC Sports–Philadelphia, had also closely covered the controversy on the Merion Middle girls' basketball team that had led to Fran Dunphy, the great ex-college coach, taking over the team for the last eight games of the season. Coach Dunphy's presence had turned the girls' season around. It had also made the team something of a media sensation in Philadelphia.

Andi was grateful—especially for what Jeff's dad and his colleagues had done during soccer season—but enough was enough. She was a sixth grader. She didn't need any more TV time.

And she certainly didn't need an agent.

She was about to tell Jeff that when his mom spoke up.

"You know, Andi, I get where you're coming from," she said. "But I'll bet you aren't the only underage athlete this guy is chasing around. In fact, I'll bet he's not the only agent doing this sort of thing. I think, at the very least, you should let Jeff's dad poke around and see what he finds out."

Andi wondered if Jeff's mom might be right. Still, she wasn't sure.

"I hear what you're saying," she said. "There might be a story here that has very little to do with me." She paused. "Let me talk to my parents tonight and see what they think."

Mrs. Michaels was making a left turn and didn't answer for a moment.

"I think that's fair enough," she said finally. "Jeff, give Andi the card. If her parents want to find out more about this guy, maybe they should make the first call."

"My parents won't want to know more about him," Andi said.

"Then they can toss the card or you can give it back to Jeff. Point is, it should be your decision all the way."

Andi liked the way Mrs. Michaels thought. It was easy to see why Jeff was the person he was: He had smart, thoughtful parents.

They pulled into the Carillos' driveway.

"What do you think you're gonna do?" Jeff asked as Andi was pulling her backpack and racquet case out of the wayback.

"Probably just show up for practice tomorrow," Andi said. "That's plenty for me."

JEFF AND ANDI DIDN'T HAVE ANY MORNING CLASSES together, but they almost always sat with each other at lunch along with a handful of friends they had played soccer and basketball with during the fall and winter.

Which is why, with a half-dozen people seated around the table, Jeff was surprised when Andi put her tray down and announced, "Have I got a story to tell."

This wasn't Andi's way—calling attention to herself. Everyone got quiet quickly.

She began by filling the others in on what had happened after the match the previous day, glancing at Jeff on occasion as if checking to see if he had already told any of the others the story.

He hadn't and was glad of it, since he knew his face always gave him away when he was hiding something.

Jeff clicked in when Andi started talking about what had taken place after she'd gotten home.

"My parents were *not* happy," she said. "My mom kept saying, 'She's *eleven* and they're coming after her. *Eleven!*'

"So, my dad called an agent he knows, a guy named Tom Ross, who has been around tennis forever. They went to law school together. He said Ross laughed when he said he was shocked about what had happened. Ross told him *every* big sports agency has young, wannabe agents they send out to scout young players, really young players—like me.

"My dad called Walters's company today and, sure enough, he's not an agent, he's what they call a rover. He has no authority to sign people or offer anyone anything. All he does is report back to the real agents if he sees someone who has potential."

"That's all he could see yesterday. He ignored me completely," Jeff said with a smile.

"Not funny," Andi said, giving him a look. "I don't want to deal with him or any other agent again."

It was Danny Diskin, who had played both soccer and basketball with Andi and Jeff, who spoke up next. "So, why doesn't your dad just tell baby-agent-wannabe to buzz off?" he asked.

Andi smiled. "He did. Sent him an email this morning."

"Did he hear back?" Lisa Carmichael said.

Andi shook her head. "Dad sent it just before we left for school, so I have no idea if he's heard from him since."

Jeff spooned some ice cream. "If what my dad says about agents is true, they won't give up that easily," he said. "You guys might think your dad's note was the end. I'm betting it's just the beginning."

Andi still hadn't eaten any lunch at all. Jeff suspected her pasta was getting cold. "Well, if they don't go away," she said, "I know where to find you. And your dad."

There was no sign Friday afternoon of Tad Walters or anyone who looked like an agent—as in, overtly over-dressed for a kids' tennis match—when Merion traveled to Haverford College to play Haverford Middle School.

The Little Squirrels—the nickname for both the high school and the middle school came from the college—used Haverford's tennis courts for their home matches. They were in a leafy corner of the campus, the trees surrounding the six courts providing comfortable shade on an unseasonably warm day, the temperatures rising into the mid-70s.

"Feels like baseball season," Jeff said to Andi as they got off the bus and looked around.

"It *is* baseball season," Andi answered. "Yesterday was opening day, remember?"

Jeff remembered. The Phillies had opened on the road, beating the Washington Nationals in Washington with Bryce Harper hitting two mammoth home runs.

Jeff's dad hadn't made the trip to DC, the theory being that opening day in Philly—which was the following Tuesday against the Mets—was a lot more important than opening day on the road.

Because Haverford had six courts, all the singles matches were played at once. Since the matches were set up with number one girls on Court One and number one boys on Court Two, Jeff and Andi were playing next to each other. The coaches had made no lineup changes, since everyone except the boys' doubles team had won on Tuesday.

Jeff's match was against a kid named Neil Olander, a lefty who hit both his forehand and backhand with two hands. Olander was tall and had a serve that was tough to read, perhaps because Jeff didn't have much experience playing lefties and the spin on Olander's serve felt backward to him. When he expected the ball to jump to his forehand, it went to his backhand—and vice versa.

He dropped the first set 6–3 and, as he and Olander changed ends, he noticed Andi shaking hands with her opponent. He could see on the little scoreboard on the side of the court that Andi had won 6–0, 6–1. He figured she'd be upset about dropping a game.

In the second set, Jeff began to get a feel for Olander's serve and broke him twice, winning the set, 6–1.

After a consultation with his coach—totally legal at this level—Olander returned for the third set and began aiming everything at Jeff's backhand. It wasn't a bad strategy: Jeff had far more power on the forehand side.

As Jeff walked to receive serve, leading 5–4, he heard a voice hissing at him from the trees behind the court.

"Move him in, drop shot him," the voice said. "He doesn't like going near the net. Get him there."

It was Andi. She had apparently walked behind the court to get his attention. Only the coaches were allowed to actually come on court during changes to talk to players.

Olander's first serve took a high hop and Jeff barely touched it as it bounced to the backstop. It was 15–love. Can't bring him in if you can't get your racquet on the ball.

Jeff took a step back and was waiting for the next spinning, high-hop serve. He banged it into the corner and Olander's backhand floated a little as it came back. Jeff was tempted to crush it, but hearing Andi's voice in his head, he hit a drop shot instead.

Olander got to it—barely—and was standing at the net helplessly as Jeff's forehand whizzed past him.

Andi had been right. Jeff got a second serve and hit it right up the middle. Olander slammed it back and Jeff played another drop shot. This one was so good that Olander never moved. Two points from match.

Clearly tight now, Olander double-faulted. Match point. He took something off his first serve to make sure he didn't have to face the possibility of choking on his second serve, and Jeff sliced his backhand to Olander's backhand. The ball floated back. This time, Jeff didn't bother with a drop shot. He closed, crushed a forehand into the corner, and turned to raise a fist to Andi before going to net to shake hands.

"Your friend back there told you to drop me, didn't she?" Olander said, forcing a smile.

"Anything wrong with that?" Jeff said.

Olander shook his head. "Wish she were coaching me, that's all," Olander said. "She's got an amazing sense of the game. Jamie Paulsen's good. She only got one game off her."

"Jamie must be very good," Jeff said. Then, quickly, he added, "Oh, Andi's got a boyfriend."

Olander shook his head. "I'll bet she does," he said. "I'll bet she does."

Merion ended up winning the match, 5–3. Jeff was almost disappointed when the girls' doubles team clinched the victory. Even though the coaches had never talked about it, he was guessing that if the match had to go to a mixed doubles tiebreaker at 4–4, that he and Andi would have been paired together, since they were each playing number one singles.

The teams did their cheers for one another and then went through a handshake line. Jeff noticed that Olander was holding on to Andi's handshake and talking to her. He saw Andi smile and glance in Jeff's direction. He was pretty certain that Olander hadn't taken Jeff at his word about Andi having a boyfriend.

"What was that about?" he asked as they gathered their racquets and towels to head for the bus.

Andi shrugged. "He asked me if I'd like to go to a movie sometime," she said. "I told him thanks, but no thanks."

She smiled. "Then he said that you'd told him I had a boyfriend."

"What'd you say?" Jeff said, semi-panicked.

"I backed you up," she answered. "He asked me if it

was serious. I said, 'I'm eleven, how serious can it be?' That kind of freaked him out. He's fourteen. He said he figured I was thirteen. He started apologizing."

Jeff knew that Andi could easily pass for thirteen if she wanted to because she was tall. He couldn't really blame Olander—although he was a little annoyed that Neil hadn't believed him when he said Andi had a boyfriend.

"I'm not thrilled that he didn't believe me," Jeff said.

"Why?" she answered. "You *were* lying."

She had a point.

"You'd better be careful," she added. "People might think you were jealous or something."

Jeff didn't think his face could get any redder. His friend really did have an amazing sense of the game—on and off the court.

7

JEFF AND ANDI DECIDED TO MEET TO PLAY AGAIN ON
Saturday. Jeff didn't mind the idea of getting crushed
again, especially if they ended up at Andy's for pizza
when they were finished.

He was feeling a good deal more secure about his
game than he had been the last time they had played.
The fact that he was playing number one singles and
was 2–0 had a lot to do with it.

So did knowing that Andi wasn't just a good player,
but a nationally ranked player who had actually drawn
the attention of at least one agent-wannabe.

They warmed up for longer than normal, Andi pointing out ways Jeff could improve his game.

"You saw what happened yesterday when you
stopped trying to crush every shot," she said. "You
don't have to attack on every point. Even Federer

mixes it up and his ground strokes are a little better than yours."

"Yeah, but mine are better than Djokovic," he said, laughing at the notion that anyone would compare his tennis game to Roger Federer or Novak Djokovic in any context. The two men combined had won forty major championships. Jeff was 2–0 playing middle school tennis. Not quite the same thing.

When they started to play, Jeff did try to mix up his shots; drawing Andi to the net on occasion, taking something off both his forehand and backhand. It helped. He only lost the first set, 6–3.

They decided to take a break and sat on a bench set up where an umpire's chair might be if the court had one. It was a warm morning and Jeff was wishing he'd worn a cap to protect himself from the sun the way Andi had.

"You're better today," Andi said. "Some of it is mixing up your shots, but you're moving better, too. I think it's because—"

"Good morning, Andi," a voice said behind them.

Surprised, they both looked around. Standing behind them was Tad Walters with a wide smile on his face. For an instant, Jeff didn't recognize him. He looked nothing like he had looked at the match on Tuesday.

Instead of the pinstripe suit, he was dressed as if

he was on his way to play tennis: blue Under Armour–logoed tennis shirt, white shorts, and sneakers. He looked as if he'd passed on shaving that morning. Part of the casual look, Jeff guessed.

Andi found her voice first.

"What in the world are you doing here?" she said.

Jeff caught up before Walters could answer. "How'd you know where we were?" he said.

Walters smiled. "A good reporter never reveals his sources," he said. "You should know that, kid, given what your father does."

"*You* are not a reporter," Jeff shot back. "Far from it." All the while he was wondering how Walters knew what his father did—although it certainly wouldn't be tough to find out.

"Either way, I just wanted to find a quiet minute or two with Andi without so many people around," Walters said. "I'm not trying to cause any trouble at all. I just want her to know—"

"I don't need to know anything about you," Andi said. "I already know enough. You're not even a real agent, you're just a scout or something."

"I'm a rover," Walters said, clearly not fazed. "And I never said I was an agent. You just assumed I was one because of who I work for."

Jeff realized he was right about that. He'd said he worked for ProStyles but had never said he was an agent. That didn't make him any less sleazy in Jeff's mind.

Walters was still talking. "I know you're much too young to need an agent, but your notion that your parents can represent you when you're ready to turn pro is naïve. I'm sure they can read a contract, but you're going to need an agency that knows who has money, which corporations need a young player, and how to get the most money possible for you. If you let your parents do that, you could leave millions of dollars on the table."

"Millions?" Jeff said, knowing as soon as he said it that he shouldn't have opened his mouth.

"Yes, Michaels, millions," Walters answered calmly.

"I don't *care*," Andi said. "I don't want to turn pro or make millions or have an agent. I just want to play tennis and have fun."

"Why not play tennis, have fun, *and* make millions?" Walters persisted. "I may not be an agent, but in my job I see a *lot* of young players. I know my tennis. I know who has the potential to be a star and who doesn't. You, young lady, have star potential in bushels."

Jeff thought he saw Andi blush just a little. That didn't mean, however, that she was charmed one tiny bit.

"Look, Mr. Walters—"

"Call me Tad."

"Whatever," she said. "I have no interest in being a professional tennis player right now. My plan is to go to college—which is still six years away—and, if I still love the game after I graduate and I'm good enough, *maybe* I'll take a crack then. But not before then. So please, go pick on some other kids, but not on me."

"I'm not *picking* on you at all," he said. "I'm trying to tell you that you have the talent to be very rich in the not too distant future. Not *now*—obviously. But the time to cash in for a tennis player, especially an attractive female tennis player, is at fifteen, sixteen. After that, the corporate opportunities dry up fast."

"So, if she's really good at twenty-one, no one's going to be interested in her?" Jeff said.

"Not until and unless she wins a major, no," Walters said. "She'll be too old."

"Chris Evert didn't turn pro until she finished high school at least," Andi said. "She was eighteen. Over the hill, according to you."

"She also made the U.S. Open semis when she was sixteen and then won *eighteen* majors," Walters said. "You win eighteen majors, sure, absolutely, you'll make plenty of money."

He wasn't backing down, and he knew his tennis history, Jeff had to give him that. But Jeff knew Andi wasn't going to be swayed.

"Look, Mr. Walters—"

"Tad," he said again.

"Whatever," she repeated. "I have your card. If for any reason at all my parents feel the need to talk to you, we know where to find you."

That—finally—seemed to satisfy Walters. "Good, great," he said. "Think Coco Gauff."

"Maybe I'll think Jennifer Capriati while I'm at it," Andi said.

Jeff didn't know the name. Walters just smiled, waved, and walked away.

"Ready to play again?" Jeff said, figuring the sooner they moved on the better.

Andi shook her head. "I'm done. Let's go get some pizza. Guy makes me wish I'd never picked up a racquet."

"So who is Jennifer Capriati?" Jeff asked as they walked back to Andi's house.

Andi laughed. "She was supposed to be the next Chris Evert when she turned pro right after Evert retired. She was thirteen . . ."

"She turned pro when she was thirteen?"

Andi nodded. "Oh yeah. She could play. Made the semis at the French Open and the U.S. Open that year right after she turned fourteen."

"And?"

"And her father pushed her so hard that she burned out and quit before she was eighteen. Looked like she was going to be a washout. She actually came back a few years later—without dad around—and won three majors. But she went through hell for years because she was pushed too hard too fast."

"What do you think will happen to Gauff?"

"Well, at least in part because of Capriati, the women's tour now has rules on how many tournaments you can play in a year before you're sixteen. That helps, but it's no guarantee a kid—any kid—will be able to deal with all the stardom and all the money if it comes too soon. She's already talked about dealing with depression. She's seventeen!"

Andi's mom gave them a ride to the mall with the understanding that Jeff's mom would pick them up in a couple of hours. During the ten-minute ride, Andi and Jeff decided not to bring up Walters's ambush—at least for the moment. Andi was thinking perhaps one of her parents might get some kind of court order to keep him from approaching her again, but she wasn't ready to deal with all the hassles that might be involved.

She'd had to testify in court back in January because of the controversy involving the girls' basketball team at Merion Middle and, although she'd done well and things had turned out fine, she had no desire to go through anything like that again anytime soon.

She explained that to Jeff as they walked through the mall when he asked why she hadn't mentioned the rover's visit to her mom.

They ordered their usual—a six-slice pizza; four for Jeff, two for Andi—and found a table. It was 11:30 on a Saturday and the mall was getting crowded fast.

"I think it's fine not to tell your parents for now," Jeff said as he pulled a slice free. "But I don't think this guy's going to quit. His next move might be to bring in one of their big guns—you know, a real agent."

Andi watched with amusement as Jeff's eyes lit up with the first bite.

"You're right," she said as Jeff happily munched away. "He might lay low for a little while, but he'll be back one way or another. Which is why—for once—I think getting your dad involved might be the right thing to do."

Jeff was clearly surprised when she said this—with good reason. Even though Tom Michaels and NBC Sports–Philadelphia had played a key role in helping Andi get on the soccer team and had also followed the story of her basketball team—which had involved ousting an officious coach and replacing her with Philadelphia legend Fran Dunphy—Andi had never wanted the publicity.

Her closest friends on the basketball team—Lisa Carmichael, Eleanor Dove, and Maria Medley—had taken to calling her "TV troublemaker Andi Carillo." It was good-natured, but Andi wasn't the least bit comfortable with it.

Now, though, she thought some publicity—even just potential publicity—might help.

"Instead of waiting for this guy to make his next move which, like you said, *is* going to happen, *we* make the next move," she said.

"How?" Jeff said as Andi pulled out her phone and started googling something.

"Your dad calls ProStyles. He doesn't talk to Walters, he's a nobody, he finds out who Walters reports to and talks to him. He might even call Donald Johnston the third. That'll get their attention."

"Who in the world is Donald Johnston the third?" Jeff asked.

"He is, to quote their website, 'the president and founder of ProStyles. One of the most respected men in the sports industry.'"

"A respected agent?" Jeff said. "That's funny. But I doubt he'll want any kind of story about one of his employees stalking eleven-year-olds. Because we know you're not the only one they're chasing around."

Andi could tell Jeff liked the idea of getting his dad involved. He even put down his second slice of pizza for a moment to think about it.

"What if they say there's nothing to it, that Walters

was acting on his own and they know nothing about it? Then there's no story."

It was now Andi's turn to put down her pizza. "What do you think the chances are that's the truth?" she asked.

He picked up slice number three and smiled.

"About the same as your chances of getting a third slice," he said.

"So, zero," she said, sort of wishing that wasn't the case.

"Yeah," he said. "I'd say that's exactly right."

8

THE BALL WAS NOW IN JEFF'S COURT. MORE SPECIFICALLY, Tad Walters's card was in his hands.

He was surprised that his dad was the one who picked him and Andi up at the mall. Reading his mind, his dad said, "All the pro teams are out of town. I have the day off. My plan is for you and me to watch the regional finals tonight."

Jeff had almost forgotten that this was elite eight weekend, that four games in four different places would decide who would make it to the following weekend's Final Four, which was to be played in New Orleans.

In another year, the NCAA regionals would be played in the Wells Fargo Center, which was directly across the parking lot from where the Spectrum had once stood. Jeff was excited about that. The last time the tournament had been in Philadelphia—2016—he'd been six and too young to go to night games.

"Let me know what happens later," Andi said as she got out of the car.

"You got it," Jeff said.

"What happens with what later?" Jeff's dad asked as they pulled away.

For once, Jeff didn't have to tell him it was no big deal, or he couldn't talk about it. He laid the whole story out for him, finishing just as they pulled into the garage.

Tom Michaels had been a reporter for a long time, and he knew not to interrupt someone when they were telling a story. Now, as they walked into the kitchen, he said: "First of all, Andi's father's friend—the agent?—is right that this is nothing new.

"But I will say this, eleven *is* young, even for tennis. Andi must be really good if someone's chasing her already."

"She's very good, Dad," Jeff said. "You should come and see her play. But you really think there aren't other eleven-year-olds this guy is going after?"

"Only one way to find out," Tom Michaels said. "I've got to make some phone calls starting Monday."

"Who do you call first?" Jeff said.

His dad smiled. "Agents," he said. "If Tony doesn't object, I'll call his friend Ross first since he apparently knows tennis. Then, I'll call some of the agents I know."

"You know tennis agents?" Jeff said, surprised.

"Just one," he said. "But she'll know other tennis agents to talk to and my other guys will know who the bad guys are in the tennis business and can point me there."

"You can tell the bad guys from the good guys?" Jeff asked.

"No," his dad said. "There are bad guys and worse guys in agenting. No good guys. Which means, there will be plenty of guys out there willing to rat out this Walters guy and any others doing this sort of thing."

Jeff had a thought that made him smile.

"What are you smiling about?" his dad asked.

"I was just thinking: What if it turns out Walters is one of the guys who's just bad, not worse?"

"In the agent business, that's certainly possible," Tom Michaels said. "In fact, it's very possible."

9

PRACTICE ON MONDAY WAS CUT SHORT BECAUSE IT STARTED to rain at about 4:30. They played for a few more minutes before the rain became a downpour and the coaches ordered everyone inside.

There was a rarely used lounge area between the boys' and girls' locker rooms with soda machines, a couple of couches, some chairs, and a desk with a laptop computer on it.

Usually, players were either coming or going from the locker room and didn't stop in the lounge except perhaps for a soda or to check something out online.

Now, Coach Foster and Coach O'Grady sat everybody down, while the managers—one for the boys, one for the girls—went into the locker rooms to grab towels for everyone. Andi was dying for a Coke, but her wallet was in her locker. Plus, Coach Foster opened the meeting by saying, "This will only take a minute or two. Then you guys can all shower and get home to do homework.

"Those of you who have your cell phones in your racquet bags, take a minute to text your parents if you need to let them know practice ended early."

As soon as Andi powered her phone on, she saw a text from her dad. *Raining. Do you need me to come early?*

She looked at the time on the phone: it was 4:45. *How about 5:15?* she responded. Normal pickup was six.

Almost instantly, her father shot back a thumbs-up emoji. He'd been watching his phone.

Coach Foster waited another minute and then went through the itinerary for the trip the next day to Bryn Mawr Tech—which was one of the other schools that had its own courts.

When he was finished, Coach O'Grady said: "Just so you all know, this isn't like basketball. They're *good* at tennis. In fact, they won their opener against Haverford by the same score we did: 5–3. So be ready to play."

The Techies were definitely *not* good in basketball. The Merion Middle boys' and girls' teams had beaten them easily, which fit with their reputation as the "nerd school" in the league. Apparently though, nerds could play good tennis.

Coach Foster held up his hand to quiet the giggles and whispers that had followed Coach O'Grady's comment.

"One other thing," he said. "We've decided to shake the lineup up a little bit tomorrow. This is *not* a reflection on anyone's play, we just want to shift a couple things around so we can be prepared to put our best lineup out when we get deeper into the season.

"On the girls' side, we're going to move Jane Blythe to third singles and put Mindy Garceau with Patty Gerson for doubles. Mindy, we just think with your height you can be very effective in doubles."

That made sense to Andi, especially since Garceau had lost her singles match against Haverford. Her serve and her height at the net would work well in doubles.

The other change Coach Foster announced was something of a surprise. "We're going to flip the number one and two spots on the boys' side," he said. "Jeff, this has nothing to do with your play, we just want to see how this might shake out for down the road."

Andi looked at Jeff and could see he wasn't at all happy. The meeting broke up a couple of minutes later and the boys and girls headed for their respective locker rooms. Andi wanted to talk to Jeff, but he made a beeline for the boys' side of the building.

As soon as she was inside, she texted him: *U OK?*

His answer came right back. *No. Not fair. I'm 2–0. I'll call you later.*

K.

Jeff resorting to one letter answers was unusual to say the least.

They talked it through on the phone that night. "I don't think this is a big deal," Andi said. "I really think the coaches want to experiment a little."

"Easy for you to say," Jeff said. "No way you won't play number one."

Andi knew he was right. "I know, I'm sorry," she said. "I didn't mean to sound as if you shouldn't be frustrated. All you can do is go out, whip their number two guy tomorrow and go from there."

"Yeah," he said. "Maybe next match I'll get to whip the number three guy."

They hung up a moment later. On occasion, Andi forgot how competitive Jeff was. He was a good athlete—not a great one—but he hated losing. To him, being dropped to number two—regardless of the reason—was like losing.

The next day was the first of April, but no one on the Merion Middle School tennis team was in a mood to fool around.

It was cloudy and chilly and the temperature was

in the fifties when they got off the bus. Bryn Mawr Tech had six courts—highly unusual, but since the middle school and the high school were right next to each other, they had clearly been built to be used by both the middle school and high school teams.

As had been the case at Haverford, all six single matches were held at the same time. The boys were on courts 1 and 3 and 5, the girls on 2 and 4 and 6.

That meant Andi, on court 2, was right next to Jeff, who was on court 3.

As they walked out to warm up, Andi realized she had played her opponent before. Her name was Carolyn Fiore and she was a year older than Andi. They had played the previous summer because Fiore hadn't yet turned thirteen, and Andi had won a tough match, 7–6, 6–4.

When they shook hands before starting to warm up it looked to Andi as if Fiore had grown since they had last played. They'd been about the same height—at least in Andi's memory—and now Fiore was clearly a couple of inches taller.

"This isn't going to be easy," she said to herself as she pulled off her sweats to start the match.

She was right. Fiore hadn't just added height, she'd added power. Her first serve was tough to get back into play, and her second serve had a big topspin kick that put Andi on the defensive on almost every point. Fiore also often attacked the net—rare in a teen player—off both her first and second serves.

She was a different player than the one Andi had faced nine months earlier—and a better one.

Both players held serve until 5–all in the first set. Fiore held for 6–5 and then, at 30–all in the next game, surprised Andi by attacking the net off a second serve. Andi's forehand floated just enough that Fiore was able to reach it with a forehand volley that she angled so sharply Andi had no chance to get to it.

Set point. Andi's blasted first serve went long. Trying to make sure Fiore didn't come in again, she tried to do too much with her second serve, and it twisted wide.

Double fault. First set to Fiore, 7–5.

Andi found herself thinking, "I'm glad we won't be in the same age group this summer," when she heard someone shouting at her: "Pick your head up, Andi. You're better than this!"

It was Jeff. She had been so focused on her drawn-out first set, that she hadn't even noticed that the court next to hers was now occupied by four doubles players warming up. She had noticed early on that Jeff was up 4–0 when she had switched ends with Fiore. She now assumed he had won easily.

Fiore quickly held serve to start the second set. Andi took a deep breath as she walked past her to switch sides of the net. She could hear Jeff yelling encouragement, but the louder voice she was hearing most at that moment was her own, coming from inside her head.

"You aren't going to win every match easily," she was telling herself. "Dig in. You're better than she is, you just have to figure her out. *Think*, Andi, *think*."

She realized she hadn't tried anything different in the first set, content to stand on the baseline and exchange ground strokes. That wasn't good enough.

She changed her serve: abandoning her straight power first serve and serving high topspin, aiming for Fiore's backhand every chance she got. She took something off her fastball—especially on the forehand side—to force Fiore in, but not all the way in. She began to get her into no-man's land, making her come to the service line to return her shots.

Fiore was caught off guard by the sudden change in tactics. At 1–all, Andi finally broke her. She served out the set at 6–4.

Now it was Fiore's turn to change tactics. She began dinking the ball to get Andi to the net, which she knew was not the younger player's strength. There were four service breaks in the third set—there had been two total in the first two sets—and, when Andi held at 5–6, the match came down to a tiebreak. By now, all the other singles matches were over, and the players were gathered around the fence at the back of the court cheering the two players on.

As she walked back to receive serve to start the tie-break, Andi hissed at Jeff, "What's the match score?"

"We're down 3–2," Jeff said. "We *need* your point."

Andi nodded. *Okay*, she thought. *Let's find out what you're made of right now, Andi.*

Down 5–6 in the tiebreak, she saved a match point with a perfect forehand pass down the line after Fiore came in behind a first serve. Fiore held up her racquet, the tennis player's salute for a good shot.

She stayed back on the next point and Andi, who had tried exactly one drop shot all day, decided to try one. It was perfect. Fiore was standing way back to slug her ground strokes and couldn't get close to it.

Now it was 7–6, match point on Andi's racquet. She bounced the ball a few extra times thinking about what she wanted to do with the serve.

Finally, she served, not down the middle of the court or toward the doubles' alley, but right in the center of the service box—right at Fiore's body. Fiore had been leaning left, expecting a wide serve, and she almost had to jump to get out of the way as the ball bounced directly at her. She awkwardly pushed at the ball and it floated toward the net, Andi rushing in to get to it.

But there was no need. The ball hit the net tape weakly and bounced back on Fiore's side.

Game, set, match—Andi had won!

She could hear her teammates cheering wildly as she stood at the net waiting to shake hands with Fiore.

"Great match," she said, suddenly exhausted.

"You too," Fiore said, putting an arm around her. "I'm glad you won't be in my age group this summer."

"Me too," Andi said with a grin. It was about as satisfying a win as she could ever remember.

10

FORTUNATELY FOR ANDI—AND MERION—BOTH DOUBLES
teams won, meaning that Merion won the match, 5–3.
A 4–4 tie would have meant playing a mixed doubles
match and Andi wasn't sure she'd have had the energy
needed to play again—although she never would have
backed down from playing the match.

It turned out Jeff had won, 6–1, 6–1. Bryn Mawr had
won the other two girls' matches and Gary Morrissey
had lost at number one boys' singles. That accounted
for Bryn Mawr's three points.

"I watched the third set of Gary's match," Jeff quietly told Andi on the bus ride home. "I'd have beaten
the guy in straight sets."

He was still brooding about being dropped to number two.

"So, you got an easy win instead," she said. "I'm

sure the coaches noticed both matches. The important thing is we won, right?"

He was silent for a moment, and Andi suspected he was thinking about whether to answer honestly or just give her the easy, "All that matters is that we won."

He gave her both answers. "Of course, I'm glad we won," he said. "But I still don't think it was fair for me to be dropped to playing number two."

Andi sighed. Boys' egos, it seemed, were different than girls' egos. Mindy Garceau hadn't complained at all about being dropped from number three singles to playing doubles.

"Coaches are probably right," she'd said. "I am fine at singles but I'm very good at doubles."

On the other hand, Mindy had lost her singles match against Haverford before getting demoted. Jeff hadn't lost and had been dropped.

"I'll bet you're back at number one for the King of Prussia match Friday," Andi said to Jeff. "If not, then you have a right to ask the coaches what's going on."

Jeff said nothing. Andi sighed. She sat back, closed her eyes and replayed the final points of her tiebreak against Carolyn Fiore.

Fiore's words as they shook hands at the net brought a smile to her face: "I'm glad you won't be in my age group this summer."

That was a real compliment, one she would enjoy for a while.

Jeff was still in a bad mood when he got into the car at school with his father. He had texted to say the team had won and he had won, so his father had a smile on his face as Jeff tossed his racquet bag onto the back seat.

"Nice going," his dad said as he climbed into the car.

"Dad, I played a guy I could have beaten left-handed," he said. "Hardly a big deal."

"There's an old saying in sports," his dad said. "Never throw back a win. I'll bet you're back at number one on Friday."

"You sound like Andi."

"Andi, as you know, is a very smart girl."

Jeff laughed. On that they could certainly agree.

"Anyway, I have some news that may interest you," his dad said as he pulled into traffic—lots of it—on the Schuylkill Expressway. "I made some calls today about Andi's friend Tad Walters."

Jeff instantly forgot about the match.

"What'd you find out?" he said.

"Three very important things," his dad said. "One, he's not as young as you guys thought. He's actually close to forty. Second, he's been doing this a long time, although he tends to focus apparently on girls who are thirteen and fourteen. Third, every major sports agency has at least one of him—some have more."

"You mean they all have guys whose entire job is to convince girls to turn pro and sign with their company?"

"Pretty much," his dad said. "The scouting part is the most important actually because the agencies don't want to sign girls who turn out not to be good enough to make them money. If that happens too often, it means the agency is wasting both time and money on a player. You bring too many duds to your agency and you'll find yourself out of a job.

"Walters is apparently good at what he does—so good, in fact, that he's had chances to become an agent and turned them down because he gets paid on a percentage basis."

"What's that mean?"

"It means if a girl he recommends and signs makes, say, a million bucks for the agency in a year, he gets ten percent of it—*plus* his regular salary. You sign the next Coco Gauff or Bianca Andreescu and you can get very rich, very quickly."

"Even though you don't make the deals for the player?"

"Exactly. As soon as the girl signs, someone else

takes over and you go looking for the next potential star."

"Why don't they recruit boys?"

"They do—on occasion. Very few boys are ready to compete on the pro level before they're seventeen or eighteen—if then. Girls routinely are ranked in the Top 20 when they're fifteen or sixteen. They start winning majors, and the younger they are, the more popular they are with corporate America and with television."

"Wasn't Rafael Nadal very young when he won his first major?"

"Yes. He was nineteen. But he was an exception. Serena Williams was sixteen. *Most* great female players win their first major before they're twenty. Others get close but are still marketing stars."

"Like Jennifer Capriati."

His father gave him a look. "I didn't know you knew that story. But yes. Gabriela Sabatini was another and, more recently, Eugenie Bouchard. Sabatini *did* win one major, but it was five years after she'd become a star. Bouchard's never won one."

"But is Andi *that* good?"

"I honestly don't know. It's much too soon to tell. But I will tell you this much. I talked to agents from five different agencies today."

"And?"

"And they all knew her name."

"At eleven."

"At eleven, yes."

"Pretty scary."

Tom Michaels shook his head as they finally pulled off the Schuylkill. "Not pretty scary," he said. "*Very* scary."

11

JEFF WASN'T SURE WHETHER HE SHOULD SHARE WHAT HIS father had told him with Andi. He was afraid she might freak out. Plus, the fact that five agencies beyond Pro-Styles had her on their radar didn't mean they were going to pursue her the way Tad Walters had.

And yet, he was torn. After all, it was *her* life they were talking about and she had as much right to know what his dad had learned as he did—more right, in fact.

He was still deciding exactly what to say when Andi sat down at their lunch table and said: "I don't know what your dad found out, but I think he needs to do something on this sooner rather than later."

"Really?" Jeff said, surprised. "I thought you were pulling for later—or never."

"I was," she said. "But I got two emails last night."

"Walters again?" he said, which made sense and disgusted him all at once.

"No!" she said. "Two other guys from two other agencies. They were both 'invitations,' for my parents and me to meet with them—for lunch or dinner. One suggested dinner at Capital Grille. That was weird enough but then the other said he'd heard I really liked Andy's Pizza and perhaps we could all meet there."

"How in the world did someone find out you like Andy's Pizza?" Jeff asked, astonished.

"I don't know," Andi said. "But it gives me the creeps. Makes me think someone might have been following us."

That sounded crazy to Jeff, but he didn't have any other theories on how anyone might have known about their trips to Andy's.

Lisa Carmichael joined them—along with Eleanor Dove and Maria Medley, Andi's teammates during basketball season. Andi told the three of them about the emails.

"Who'd they come from?" Eleanor asked, a question Jeff hadn't gotten the chance to ask.

"One was from something called New Advantage," Andi said. "I think there used to be a group called Advantage, but this is different. The other one was Aces International. As the name says, they pretty much specialize in tennis."

"How in the world did they get your email?" Maria asked.

"Probably the same way they found out she likes Andy's," Eleanor said.

She turned to Jeff, pointing a finger at him. "If they know about Andy's, they know you go there with her a lot," she said. "I'll bet you're going to hear from them at some point."

"Why?" Jeff asked.

"They'll try to recruit you to recruit her," Maria said, clearly seeing where Eleanor was going. "They might even offer you money to help—more if you deliver. Happens in basketball all the time."

"Are you saying they might try to turn Jeff into a street agent?" Lisa said, and everyone laughed. They were all basketball fans and knew that street agents abounded, especially at the high school level where colleges and shoe companies were willing to use anyone they could find to get close to an athlete.

"How much do you think I can get?" Jeff asked, laughing.

"If someone approaches you, I think you should find out," Andi said, not smiling even a little bit.

"What in the world are you talking about?" Jeff asked.

"I'm saying, let's find out all we can about these guys. One way to do it is to find out if they're actually willing to try to turn you—or anybody else—into a street agent."

"Spoken like a true reporter," Lisa said.

"Hey, I'm the one who's the son of a reporter," Jeff said.

"Well then," Andi said. "Be ready to go to work when the time comes."

Eleanor proved to be prophetic. Jeff hadn't taken two steps out of the locker room that afternoon on his way to practice, when a man in an expensive Nike outfit jumped off the bench outside the locker room and stepped in front of him, big smile on his face, hand out.

"Peter Singer," he said as Jeff reluctantly shook his hand. "You're Jeff Michaels, right?"

Jeff was tempted to tell him he was someone else, but curiosity and Andi's comment about being a reporter stopped him.

"I'm Jeff," he said. "What do you want?"

He realized he was being brusque, which was not the best way to get the guy to feel comfortable. Except the guy didn't seem to notice.

"Jeff, I work for New Advantage," he said. "We're the fastest growing sports agency in the country."

"How exactly do you measure that?" Jeff asked,

then realized he was straying far from the important topic in order to be a wise guy.

"Huh?" Peter Singer said. Then he recovered: "We've added more employees and clients than anyone in the last year. Good question, though. You're obviously a smart young man."

Let the butt-kissing begin, Jeff thought.

"Anyway, you can probably guess why I wanted to talk to you," he continued, looking around as other kids walked past, giving them looks as they headed to practice for various spring sports. Jeff wondered if Andi was already at the courts or would come walking by at any minute. It seemed clear that Singer was thinking the same thing.

"Look, I know you have to get to practice," he said, producing a business card in the same magical way that Tad Walters had. "Stick that in your shorts. We really believe we can do good things for your friend Andi Carillo. All we want is a chance to talk to her. We think you can help us with that."

"Why would I do that?" Jeff asked.

Singer smiled. "First, because you're her friend and it would be a good thing for her. Second, because you help us out, we'll help you out."

Jeff was tempted to ask exactly how he intended to do that, but knew he had to get to practice and was about to be late.

"I gotta go," he said, not closing any doors. Although, what he really wanted to say was, *"Leave her alone!"*

"I understand," Singer said. "We'll be in touch."

Jeff had no doubt about that. Singer turned and walked quickly to the circle where parents normally picked up their kids after practices were over. A car was waiting there.

He climbed into the passenger seat and the car—some kind of blue SUV—roared away.

Andi had opened the locker room door a couple of minutes earlier and had seen Jeff talking to the guy in the expensive sweats. She quickly ducked back inside and stood with the door a crack open, moving out of the way as other girls pushed past her, giving her funny looks.

As soon as he left, she opened the door and walked over to Jeff, who was staring at the guy as he got into a waiting car.

"I think I know the answer, but who was that?" she said as they began walking quickly in the direction of the tennis courts.

In response, Jeff pulled the business card out of his pocket and handed it to Andi.

Andi looked at it quickly: "Peter Singer," it said on the top line. On the next line it said, "Talent Evaluator / New Advantage, Inc."

Underneath that was contact info.

"Looks like my dad nailed it," Jeff said as Andi handed him the card back.

"Did he offer you money?" she asked.

"Not directly," he said. "It was something like, 'You help us out, we'll help you out.' But the main reason I should talk to you is because that's what's best for you."

She laughed. "Of course. He's just a caring guy—like Tad Walters."

They had arrived at the courts. The rest of the team was already there.

Coach O'Grady smiled and said, "Glad you two could make it."

Jeff was pretty sure they weren't late, although he couldn't look at his phone to check. He did notice that they were the last ones to arrive.

They sat down on the bleachers, one row up from the others.

"Okay," Coach O'Grady said. "We are 3–0 now. There are two other teams that are also 3–0: Villanova, who we play in the last match of the round-robin on two occasions, and King of Prussia, who we play for the first time tomorrow."

Andi knew that Villanova was connected in some way to Villanova University, which was a few miles down the Main Line toward Philly from Merion.

Villanova High School had been around for years; Villanova Middle was relatively new.

"The good news is we're playing at home tomorrow," Coach O'Grady continued. "No bus ride to worry about.

"We're going to go with the same lineup as we went with in the Bryn Mawr match. That was a good team, best team we've faced so far. I suspect King of Prussia's better than Bryn Mawr. Coach Foster and I think there's no reason to fix what ain't broke as the old saying goes."

Jeff's hand was up in the air instantly. Before Coach O'Grady saw him, Andi pulled his hand down. She knew exactly what he was going to say.

"Not now," she whispered. "Not in front of the rest of the team."

"But—"

Coach Foster *had* seen his hand go up. "Michaels, did you want to say something?" he asked.

The entire team turned to look back at Jeff.

"No, Coach, I'm good, thanks," he said.

Coach Foster nodded and Coach O'Grady continued.

"Match with KOP will start at 3:45. We expect you here at 3:15 to get ready to play. Okay, let's everyone warm up."

Jeff was seething.

"Just practice and keep your mouth shut," Andi said as they stood up. "Complaining right now, especially after she's announced the lineup, isn't going to do you any good."

"But it's not fair . . ."

"I didn't say it was fair. Come on, let's warm up. You go out and kill their number two guy tomorrow and *then* say something."

Jeff had something to say at that moment—not later. They were now a few feet from the coaches as they walked in the direction of the courts.

Andi put a finger to her lips. Jeff sighed, zipped his mouth, and unzipped his racquet case.

12

COACH O'GRADY WAS RIGHT ABOUT KOP BEING GOOD.

Warming up, Jeff knew that Andi's notion that he would impress the coaches with another easy win playing at number two wasn't going to happen. His opponent, who introduced himself as James Mayer, was tall and had a big serve.

As the match wore on, Jeff realized that Mayer had one clear weakness: his speed. He knew that every tennis player who ever lived—even the greats—had some kind of Achilles' heel. The best male players in the game today weren't great volleyers, because the serve and volley had gone the way of black-and-white TV years ago. Serena Williams had a shaky second serve and sometimes got careless with her ground strokes. Like John McEnroe, she also had problems at times with her temper in close matches.

For kids still learning to play the game, weaknesses were easier to see. Jeff's was his backhand, which he ran around every chance he got. Mayer could stand at the back of the court and slam forehands and backhands with equal effectiveness.

He won the first set 6–4, breaking Jeff early in the set and then surviving several break points to serve the set out.

But Jeff broke him in the first game of the second set, his tactic of moving him around by aiming for corners or taking something off his shots starting to take effect.

It was a high-risk way to play: If he didn't land a ball in the corner, it went out and the point was quickly over. If he tried to bring Mayer in but let the ball hang up enough for Mayer to get to it, he was likely to see a crushed forehand or backhand go whizzing past him.

But he got more comfortable with the high-wire-without-a-net mode of play as the match wore on and he could see Mayer tiring as he made him run. He was still difficult to break, especially when he got his first serve in, but Jeff waited for his chances and pounced. He was up 3–1 in the second set when Mayer double-faulted to 30–all. When he missed his first serve on the next point, Jeff crept inside the baseline, took the second serve on the rise, and slammed a clean forehand winner. Wobbly, Mayer served another double fault and Jeff was up two breaks.

He won the set, 6–2, and then broke again to start the third set. Mayer was done. He was tired and frustrated by Jeff's tactics. He managed to hold serve once in the final set, but Jeff won easily, 6–1.

He had to admit that, even though he didn't like playing number two, it was a satisfying win. He also felt some relief when Gary Morrissey and Andi greeted him coming off court—both had already finished their matches.

Andi had won fairly easily, 6–3, 6–3, but Gary had been blasted, 6–3, 6–1 by King of Prussia's number one player, Dickie Weiss. "Be glad they kept you at number two," Gary said. "The guy's really good."

Jeff knew that he and Gary were comparable to each other and who played one and who played two was a coin toss.

"He's a sixth grader like us," Andi said, confirming what Gary had said. "But he's ranked fifth in the East. He's legit."

Jeff felt slightly relieved and slightly guilty. He was relieved he hadn't played Weiss and feeling guilty that part of him was *glad* Gary had gotten waxed, even though it wasn't good for the team and was unfair to Gary, who was a genuinely nice guy.

He changed the subject. "How are we doing?" he asked.

The coaches were at the far end of the courts watching the two remaining singles matches.

"Two–two," Andi said. "And looking like it'll be 3–3 after singles. Doubles just started a few minutes ago."

Andi's call on the singles proved to be correct. Jane Blythe rallied to win 7–6 in the third set, but Tommy Arnold, after serving for the match at 5–4 in the third, lost 7–5.

Then the girls' doubles team—which had become really tough to beat with Mindy Garceau teaming with Patty Gerson, won their match easily. But Art Schnabel and Jose Aguilar lost two close sets and went down.

The score was tied 4–4. For the first time in Merion's season, a mixed doubles match would decide which school went home with a victory.

The question for Merion was, who would play the mixed doubles? Andi and Jeff sat on the bench next to court one, surrounded by their teammates as they all waited for their coaches and the coaches from King of Prussia to confer. There was a ten-minute break before the mixed doubles began in order to give anyone who had just finished playing doubles a breather.

"They have to go with you for sure, but who will they pair you with?" Jeff said quietly to Andi.

She shook her head. "It's not a lock," she said. "Have you watched Mindy play doubles? With her serve and her height at the net, she might be better than I am."

Jeff thought about that for a moment. "Maybe," he said. "But at best it's a toss-up and she just finished playing a few minutes ago."

Andi knew that was true and she badly wanted to play. She loved high-pressure matches. She also wanted Jeff to be her partner.

"Well, if it's me, they better pair me with you."

She was about to say something else when the coaches walked over to where the players were all seated.

"We had several good options for this match," Coach Foster said. "We decided in the end to go with the players who played number one singles today—Andi and Gary. Like I said, we thought several other players deserved serious consideration, but in the end, this is the fairest way to do it.

"So, go warm up, you two, and the rest of you get ready to cheer them on."

Andi looked at Jeff, who appeared to have just been kicked in the stomach. She understood the thinking of the coaches, but also knew why Jeff would be upset. He still hadn't quite figured out why he'd been dropped from playing number one without losing a match. She hadn't figured it out, either.

King of Prussia had taken a different approach, pairing two doubles players for the mixed doubles. Given how easily Garceau and Blythe had won the girls' doubles match, Andi was a little surprised.

Because of the lateness of the hour and because all four players had already played, the match was the same kind of eight game pro set that the Merion coaches had used during tryouts.

The match didn't take very long. Both KOP players were strictly backcourters and both Andi and Gary were capable at the net. They consistently attacked, regardless of who was serving, and the KOP duo just wasn't precise enough to pass them with any consistency.

It was 4–0 before King of Prussia's boy finally held serve for 4–1. That was pretty much it. KOP didn't win another game and the set was over in little more than thirty minutes, Merion cruising to an 8–1 win. The match ended with the KOP boy serving at 30–40 and Andi crushing a forehand down the middle between the two opponents.

The pair watched the ball skip through to the back wall, then turned and jogged to the net to shake hands.

Andi was happy to get an easy win, but as everyone hugged one another before going to shake hands with all the KOP players, she could see the disappointment on Jeff's face.

"Nice going," Jeff said to her.

"We'd have won 8–0 if you had played," she said.

"We'd have won if you'd have played alone," Jeff said, clearly frustrated he hadn't had the chance to play—and star—with her.

"Next time," she said, reading his mind.

"Yeah sure," he said. "Next time."

13

ANDI TOOK HER TIME IN THE SHOWER. SHE'D TOLD HER mother to pick her up at six o'clock and, even though the mixed doubles match hadn't taken that long, she was a little bit sore and happy to spend a few minutes alone under the soothing hot water.

The locker room was empty when she finished and she put her clothes on carefully, brushed out her hair, and tied it into a wet ponytail. It was 5:55 when she walked out of the building. Her mother was never late, often early. This time, though, there was no sign of her.

Andi sat down on a sidewalk bench on the circle. It was a pretty spring day with just a few clouds and there was no one around. She knew Jeff had left quickly, still upset about not playing in the mixed doubles match. She didn't really blame him.

"I was wondering if you were ever going to come out of that locker room."

The voice came from directly behind her and was such a surprise she bolted upright off the bench. It was as if the person had been beamed down to the spot behind where she was sitting.

It was a young woman, tall and attractive, with the look of an athlete.

"Mind if I sit with you for a minute?" she said.

"My mom will be here any second," Andi said. "Who are you?"

The woman smiled. "My name is Renee Stubing. I work for New Advantage, but I'm not an agent. I just wanted to introduce myself and let you know that I have absolutely no interest in pressuring you to turn pro or go to a tennis academy or do anything other than enjoy being a really good twelve-and-under player."

Andi thought she recognized the name. Renee Stubing had played professional tennis, mostly as a doubles player, if her memory was correct. Now, she apparently worked for the same company as the guy who had accosted Jeff outside the locker room before practice on Monday.

"So, you came down here, waited around for me to shower, just to tell me that you're not an agent and you have no interest in recruiting me to sign with your company?" Andi asked. "Is that what you're telling me?"

Renee Stubing smiled.

"I never said I had no interest in recruiting you for our company—but, in reality, I don't. I want you to recruit *us*. I want you, when you're ready, to walk into our office with your parents and say, 'where do I sign?'"

"What if that time never comes?" Andi asked.

Renee Stubing shrugged. "Your loss. If you become as good a player as I think you're going to become, you're going to need representation. I know your parents are lawyers, but they know nothing about the world I live in and that you'll be living in pretty soon.

"In one sense, we're all the same—we're in business to make money and the best way for us to make money is to make money for our clients."

"But you're still different, right?" Andi said.

Renee Stubing smiled again. "It's a catch-22, Andi; you can't find out if we're different if you don't give us a chance to show you that we're different."

Andi saw her mom's car pulling up to the circle. She had to admit that Stubing's pitch was different.

"That must be your mom," Stubing said. "Do you want my card?"

That was different, too. Walters had practically thrown his card at Andi, and the guy who had accosted Jeff had done pretty much the same thing.

"Sure," she said. "Why not?"

Stubing produced the card, handed it over, and

walked away—not bothering to introduce herself to Andi's mom. Andi threw her racquet bag in the back seat and jumped into the front. She had texted her parents to let them know Merion had won 5–4 and that she and Gary Morrissey had clinched the match in mixed doubles.

"Who was that?" her mom asked as she pulled away.

"Another agent—although she said she's not an agent."

Andi's mom laughed. "They all say they're not agents—that's what Tom Ross, who IS an agent, told your father. They think the word is beneath them somehow."

"Well, I'll admit this one was different."

"How so?" her mom asked.

Andi answered the question with a question of her own. "Mom, what's a catch-22?"

Jeff hadn't even bothered to shower when the match was over. He knew he was being a lousy teammate—not enjoying the way Andi and Gary had won the mixed doubles match—but he couldn't help himself.

He had nothing against Gary; in fact, he liked him. But he was baffled at why he'd been dropped to number two without losing a match after earning the number one spot in the tryouts. When he and Gary had played, he'd beaten him 8–6. It was a close match and Jeff knew that Gary was capable of beating him on a given day.

Gary was now 0–2, playing the number one spot, and yet the coaches had gone with him in the mixed doubles match. Jeff worried that the success he'd had playing with Andi that day might lead the coaches to go with the same team in the future.

That is, unless they were watching, and realized that Andi could have teamed with one of the Michaels' family cats and won.

Since it was a Friday and his dad was working at the Phillies game that night, his mom picked him up.

"Nice win," she said as he got into the car. He'd sent a quick text with the results.

"Yeah, I guess," he said grumpily.

His mom gave him a look. "What's wrong with you?" she said. "You won your match, your team won. What's going on?"

"Did you notice the score?" he asked.

She nodded. "Yes, 5–4. It was close. What about it?"

"Mom, 5–4 means we had to play mixed doubles to decide the match," Jeff said. "I won my match, Gary lost his—*again*—and the coaches still picked him to play the mixed doubles match with Andi."

"Which, I take it, they won, right?" his mom said.

"*Yes*, they won," Jeff said, becoming aggravated.

"But they would have won if they'd both played left-handed. The other team wasn't very good at all. They won 8–1. It would have been 8–0 if I'd played instead of Gary."

"So why do you think the coaches picked Gary?" she said. "There must have been a reason."

Jeff sighed. His mom usually picked up on things faster than this.

"They said they thought it made sense to have the number one girl play with the number one boy. The thing is, I should be the number one boy!"

"But you weren't today," she said. "Your focus shouldn't be on today; it should be on what happens next."

They were home. Jeff said nothing as they got out of the car. He was beginning to wonder if *anyone* was on his side. Finally, when they walked into the kitchen from the garage he said, "So what would you do if you were me?"

"You really want to know?" she said. "You don't want to talk just to your dad about this, jock to jock?"

"I will talk about it with him," Jeff said. "But you seem to have an opinion and I'd like to hear it."

She sat down on a stool at the kitchen counter. "I think one thing your dad and I have always agreed on is that you should fight your own battles," she said.

Jeff started to answer, but she put up a hand. "In this case, though, I don't think that's the way to go."

Jeff rolled his eyes. The last thing he needed was his parents trying to intervene with a coach—or coaches.

"Mom, I don't need you guys . . ."

The hand was up again. "Jeff, you don't honestly think I'd suggest your father and I go to your coaches because you're unhappy about playing number two on a tennis team instead of number one? Or being upset because you didn't get to play mixed doubles—especially when your team *won*."

"Then what?" he said.

"Send Andi," she said. "Look, you went to Coach Crist and asked him to help when that awful girls' coach wouldn't play her during basketball season. I know she got mad at you for doing it, but you did the right thing—except you didn't tell her about it first."

"She'd have told me to mind my own business."

"Yeah, probably. And you'd have probably ignored her and done it anyway."

Jeff thought about that for a moment. She was right. Andi was never one to ask for help even when she needed it. But did he need help that much right now? Yes. No. Maybe. All three answers ran through his head.

"We're supposed to play tomorrow morning . . ."

"And then go for pizza, I know," Arlene Michaels said.

"Think about it."

That—for now—was the answer. He'd think about it. He only hoped that when he did, his head wouldn't explode with frustration.

14

JEFF AND ANDI WERE BOTH AMAZED WHEN NO ONE SHOWED up to accost them the next morning after they finished playing. Jeff won exactly one game in two sets, in large part because he was intent on hitting every shot as hard as he possibly could. He practically put a dent in the back wall because he hit it on so many occasions.

Andi said nothing until they sat down. "You know this isn't baseball, right?" she said. "Trying to hit every ball as hard as you can doesn't usually work very well."

Jeff grunted. "Yeah, I know. I guess I was taking my frustrations out on the tennis balls."

"Well, you certainly taught them a lesson."

They both laughed—which was something Jeff realized he hadn't done much in the last week.

He had decided not to ask Andi to go to the coaches on his behalf. Instead, he asked her a question: "What do you think I should do?"

"You mean about playing number two?"

"And not getting to play the mixed yesterday."

She thought about it for a moment. "The mixed isn't an issue. The coaches just decided to play Gary and me because we'd played number one singles. The issue is why you got dropped from number one singles."

"Exactly," he said. "You have any theories? Or ideas?"

"I don't really have a theory," she said. "I think Coach Foster and Coach O'Grady are trying to be fair and trying to win. I'm guessing—and I mean *guessing*—that they thought you'd be a very strong number two and Gary would do okay at number one."

"But I was 2–0 at number one," he said.

She nodded. "I know that, Jeff. Everyone in the city of Philadelphia knows that at this point."

He reddened. He knew he'd brought it up a few times.

"What's important is what happens next," she continued. "I think you wait until practice Monday and see if they switch you back. If not, then maybe you should go talk to them—not in a hostile way but to ask why you got demoted when you hadn't lost a match. You act confused—not angry."

He thought about that for a moment.

"How would you feel about asking them for me?" he said finally.

"I don't think that's a great idea," she said. "Their first question would be, 'Why isn't Jeff asking us himself?'"

"And your answer would be that he doesn't want to come across as a whiner and I happen to agree with him that he deserves to be back at number one."

She sat back and folded her arms, clearly thinking.

"I still think you have to do this yourself—if it's necessary. And if you do, take it to both coaches, not one or the other. For all we know, they might not agree. You might be preaching to the choir if you choose the wrong one."

"What's preaching to the choir?"

She rolled her eyes a little. "It means telling someone who is already singing the same tune as you to sing it with you."

"Oh." Jeff had never heard that one.

There was silence for a moment.

"What do you think they're going to do?" he asked finally.

"I don't know. The sensible thing to do is put you back at number one. I really don't think Gary would or could get upset about it at this point. But I sure as heck wouldn't want to bet my house—or my parents' house—on what they're thinking."

Jeff stood up. "Let's go get a burger."

"Excuse me?"

"Yeah, I'm getting sick of pizza."

"Seriously?"

"Absolutely not. I could eat a whole pie today."

Andi smiled. It was nice to know some things in life were guaranteed.

The pre-practice meeting on Monday started well—or so Jeff thought.

Coach Foster and Coach O'Grady had clearly decided that the best way to handle the team was for them to take turns talking to them as a group.

Today was Coach O'Grady's day. "Well, we've had a couple of close calls, but you guys have really come through when things have gotten tight," she said. "That was especially true in the mixed doubles Friday when Gary and Andi left no doubt about who the better team was, did they?"

Everyone clapped enthusiastically for Gary and Andi—including a glaring Jeff, even though he was trying to burn a hole through Coach O'Grady without her noticing.

"Coach Foster and I talked at lunch today about our lineup for tomorrow's match at Philadelphia West. Honestly, there was really only one question mark because we both believe in the old saying that you don't fix what ain't broke."

Much to his surprise, the coach looked directly at Jeff.

"Jeff Michaels, you've done everything we've asked of you. You're 4 and 0—two wins at number one and two wins at number two."

She paused and looked at Gary Morrissey, who was sitting on the front row.

"Gary, you've lost two tough matches at number one and you were great in the mixed doubles. This is a tough call for us. You're both deserving."

She paused, as if waiting for Gary or Jeff to say something. "For now, because we're winning with this lineup, we're going to keep things the same." She turned and looked at Jeff again. "I know you're disappointed, Jeff, and Coach Foster and I both understand. But there's plenty of season left, isn't there?"

Jeff wanted to point out that they had changed the lineup when they were 2–0 and, perhaps more important, when *he* was 2–0. Instead, in a voice shakier than he wanted it to be: "What about mixed doubles—if we need to play it?"

Coach Foster stepped in at that moment. "If we get to that stage again, we'll make a decision then, based on what we've seen that day."

Jeff realized that was the best answer he could hope

for under the circumstances. The other answers available were: "We'll keep going with our number ones in mixed doubles," or, "Well, given how well Gary and Andi played Friday, we'll stick with them."

The meeting broke up a minute later, everyone heading out to warm up. Gary Morrissey walked up to Jeff. "Just so you know," he said, "if I were you, I'd be upset. I want to stay at number one, and I *loved* playing mixed with Andi, but you didn't do anything to deserve getting dropped to number two."

"Thanks for saying so," Jeff said. They exchanged a fist bump. It was hard to be upset with Gary. The coaches were another story.

15

PHILADELPHIA WEST MIDDLE SCHOOL WAS A FEEDER TO nearby West Philadelphia High School—which was famous for producing great basketball teams and players.

The school was only a few blocks from the campus of the University of Pennsylvania and used the Penn tennis courts that were right next to Franklin Field and, more importantly to Jeff, about two hundred yards from the front door of the Palestra—which was college basketball's most revered arena.

Jeff had been to the Palestra with his dad on numerous occasions and loved the place. As their bus pulled up in front of both the building and the courts on 33rd Street, he could almost taste the Philadelphia pretzel that his dad always bought for him at a game.

They walked in the direction of Franklin Field—
Penn's football stadium—toward what was known as
Penn Park, which was where the tennis courts were
located. The Philly West kids were already warming up
when they got there. Jeff and Andi noticed one person
watching the warm-ups right away: Fran Dunphy.

Dunphy had coached basketball at Penn for seventeen years before moving to Temple for thirteen years.
In February, because of his friendship with Jeff's dad,
he had agreed to coach the Merion Middle School girls
for the final eight games of their season after a revolt
by the players had led to the departure of their coach.

Now he stood with his arms folded and a big smile
on his face as Andi and Jeff rushed up to greet him.

"Coach!" Andi cried. "What in the world are you
doing here?"

"Your dad told me you guys were playing here
today," he answered. "Chance to come back to my old
stomping grounds." He hooked a thumb at the Palestra. "And I don't have to go inside and risk losing a
game."

Looking at Jeff, he added, "Your dad's meeting me
here. We figured we'd watch the match, then take you
two to dinner. Andi, I checked with your mom and she
was fine with it."

Jeff and Andi looked at each other. They both
thought that was a spectacular idea.

Coach Foster was calling their names. "Michaels, Carillo, get over here and warm up."

"Get going," Coach Dunphy ordered. They complied.

Jeff saw his father arrive just as warm-ups were wrapping up. The teams gathered around their coaches and then headed for their assigned courts. There were twelve courts, meaning that all the matches would be held at once—six singles and two doubles matches. If nothing else, that would mean it would take less time to complete the competition.

Penn Park was in the shadow of Franklin Field. Coach Dunphy had explained that until the park was built, Penn's tennis courts were directly in front of the main entrance to the Palestra. This was more scenic, although the Palestra was a couple hundred yards away.

Andi played on the court that was practically on top of Franklin Field—a pretty historic place in its own right. She had actually written a social studies paper on it once, making the case that it was an important part of the city of Philadelphia's history. It had opened in 1895 and had been Penn's home football field ever since. But it had also hosted the Army–Navy game many times and been the home of the Philadelphia Eagles for more than a decade. What's more, it was at halftime of an Eagles game played there in 1968, in the midst of a snowstorm and a 3–11 season, that fans had infamously booed Santa Claus and thrown snowballs at the poor guy in the Santa suit.

In addition, Franklin D. Roosevelt had given his acceptance speech at the 1936 Democratic convention there. That fact was the reason why Mrs. Carson, Andi's fifth grade teacher, had accepted her proposal.

Jeff's match was out on court four, next to the girls' number two match between Lisa Carmichael and the Speedkids' number two female player. West Philadelphia High School's guys' and girls' teams were called the Speedboys and the Speedgirls. The junior high school's co-ed teams were the Speedkids. Jeff kind of liked that.

His opponent, who had introduced himself as Jimmy Scheuer, certainly lived up to the speed part of the nickname. He dashed all over the court, chasing down balls that Jeff was initially convinced were winners.

His problem—and the saving grace for Jeff—was his size. He was no more than five foot three and probably weighed about 110 pounds. His serve, especially the second one, floated across the net like the proverbial wounded duck.

Once Jeff figured this out, he stood halfway between the baseline and the service line for first serves and practically *on* the service line for second serves. This led to several double faults with Scheuer trying to land the ball as deep in the service box as possible. Most of the time, Jeff took either serve on the rise and then pounded it in the direction of a corner.

Scheuer ran a lot down, but not enough.

The first set was tight, Jeff winning 7–5, but Scheuer was clearly worn down in the second set and Jeff won, 6–1. He noticed Lisa shaking hands with her opponent as he and Scheuer were walking off the court, and he could tell by the look on Lisa's face that she had won.

Andi was already off the court and so were both the number three singles matches. Merion had won all five matches. "We've got a chance to sweep," Andi reported. They were ahead in both doubles matches, and Gary had just split sets.

That meant Merion had already won—there would be no mixed doubles today. Coach Dunphy and Jeff's dad came over to congratulate Jeff and Andi on their wins.

"That guy really ran down a lot of shots, didn't he?" Tom Michaels said.

"Sure did," Jeff said. "Lucky his serve was so weak."

"Hey, Mustangs, good playing," Coach O'Grady said, walking up to the group. "How about joining your teammates over at Court Two to show Gary some support?"

"What about the doubles?" Andi asked.

"They're both up a set and a break," Coach O'Hara said. "Gary's the one who could use some cheerleading."

Jeff understood. He wouldn't want to be in position to be the only one on the team to drop a match.

As they walked over, Jeff's dad announced that he and Dunphy were going to go across the street and get some coffee. "Text us when this is over, and we'll come right back to get you."

Jeff and Andi didn't mind getting ditched. The match had been decided and the two kids the men cared about had won.

The two players joined their teammates and the Philly West players to watch from a small bleacher.

The third set was tied at 2–all as they sat down.

For the next half hour, the match swayed back and forth. By 4–all, the doubles players had all finished and joined them. Merion now led 7–0.

Jeff cheered as loudly as anyone for Morrissey. He liked Gary and wanted to see him win. Plus, it was the right thing to do. But Jeff felt almost certain he'd have to be restored to playing number one if Gary lost, so cheering for him to win wasn't easy.

Gary did win. Up 6–5, the Philly West kid had a match point and went for a winner on a second serve from Morrissey—only to hit it about eight feet beyond the baseline.

"Flat-out choke," Andi said quietly.

Gary held serve for 6–6, and then, at 5–all in the tiebreak, nerves got to his opponent again. He slapped a forehand into the net and then, on match point, he twisted a second serve wide for a double fault.

The Mustangs cheered lustily for Morrissey and, after joining in the handshakes, Jeff texted his dad.

Ready when you are.

How'd Gary do? his dad responded.

Won. We swept.

Don't sound so overjoyed. On our way.

Jeff shook his head. His dad could read his tone even in a text.

Jeff and Andi let the coaches know they wouldn't be going back to school with the team and explained why.

"You sure you're okay here?" Coach Foster asked.

"We're fine," Andi said. "They'll be back in five minutes."

That seemed to satisfy him. Jeff's dad and Dunphy had introduced themselves to the two coaches before the match began, so he knew this wasn't an eleven-year-old's plot to run off and get into some kind of trouble.

The two friends sat down on an empty bench and

watched the team bus pull away. The courts were empty, except for one group of doubles players on one of the far courts.

"Well, well, looks like we got lucky, you're both here together."

Jeff and Andi looked behind them and were surprised to see Renee Stubing and her pal Peter Singer from New Advantage.

"When did you get here?" Andi said.

Stubing laughed. "Since before the matches began. We watched from over there"—she pointed to a grove of trees on the far side of the courts—"because we didn't want to distract you. Nice playing, both of you. Jeff, you're a good player."

"So, you're here to recruit me, too?" Jeff asked in as snarky a voice as he could find.

Singer laughed. "Don't flatter yourself, kid. You have the potential to play in high school. Andi has the potential to play at Wimbledon."

"Look," Andi said. "Jeff's dad and . . ."

"Fran Dunphy, we know," Stubing said. "They'll be back any minute. I met Coach Dunphy before the match started. Nice guy."

"Did you tell him you were an agent?"

"No, because I'm not an agent. I already told you that," she said. "I told him you and I were friends and I'd come to watch the matches."

"Yeah, you're not an agent," Jeff said. "And I'm not right-handed."

"Actually, even though you play right-handed, you might do well playing as a lefty," Stubing said with a smirk.

Andi saw Tom Michaels and Fran Dunphy walking in their direction and breathed a sigh of relief.

"Here comes our ride," she said, pointing in their direction. She looked directly at Stubing, who was clearly the boss. "I'm going to say this to you one last time. I really don't care what you call yourself. Call yourself the Queen of England if you want. But if you approach me again, anywhere, anytime, my parents are going to go to court and get a restraining order. They're both lawyers. It won't be difficult."

"Have you threatened Tad Walters like this?" Singer said, apparently finding his missing voice.

"Not yet," Andi said. "But I will if I have to."

Tom Michaels and Fran Dunphy arrived, both with quizzical looks on their faces.

"What's up, guys?" Jeff's dad said.

"What's up, Dad, is that these two are agents and they're harassing Andi," Jeff said.

"Agents?" Dunphy said. Turning to Stubing, he said in a tone Jeff had never heard from him before: "You said you were a friend of Andi's. I don't like being lied to, especially by an agent."

"I think I meant to say I *hope* to be a friend of Andi's," Stubing said.

Both adults were clearly angry now. "I've dealt with a lot of agents through the years," Dunphy said. "But never anyone who tried to sneak attack an eleven-year-old girl."

"You coach a lot of eleven-year-old girls?" Singer asked.

"As a matter of fact, I coached an entire team of them this winter," Dunphy answered, looking very much like he would love to take a swing at Singer. "I know agents are liars and cheats, but this is a new low."

"I think this sounds like a pretty good story," Tom Michaels said. "Why don't you two give me your cards? I'll be in touch soon."

The two agents drew back as if he'd threatened them with arrest.

"Haven't got any on me," Stubing said. "Sorry."

"It's okay, Mr. Michaels, I've got hers," Andi said.

"And I've got his," Jeff added.

"Threaten all you want," Stubing said. "We haven't broken any laws."

"Maybe not criminal laws," Mr. Michaels said. "But in your business, I suspect the court of public opinion matters a lot more."

The two agents didn't say another word. They

turned and began walking in the direction of the Palestra.

It occurred to Jeff that he and Andi had finally played mixed doubles together. And, with the help of his father and Coach Dunphy, they had won handily.

16

TOM MICHAELS AND FRAN DUNPHY DECIDED THAT, EVEN though it was a school night, Jeff and Andi deserved a good steak dinner. So, they drove into downtown Philadelphia, drove around City Hall Circle, and pulled up in front of the Capital Grille, his dad's favorite steak house—especially since The Palm, which had been a couple of blocks down Broad Street, had closed.

Andi had never been to the Capital Grille, but she'd heard her parents talk about it as one of *the* power lunch places in town. When her dad had first explained that to her, she'd had to ask: "What's a power lunch?"

Her father explained that it meant that it was a restaurant that was the place where politicians, athletes, media members, lawyers, celebrities—those who were considered important and those who considered themselves important—often met for lunch.

Jeff knew that his dad often met with sports celebrities there for interviews or just for lunch. "The main thing," he said to Andi as they walked to their table, "is that the steaks here are huge."

Andi smiled. That was more important to Jeff than to her. She just hoped the steaks were good.

They were. Andi ordered a nine-ounce fillet. Jeff asked for the eighteen-ounce strip.

Once the waiter had departed, Tom Michaels got down to business.

"Andi, I held off on pursuing this story after you were first approached because I didn't think you wanted any more publicity after what happened during soccer and basketball seasons," he said.

"I don't," Andi said.

Mr. Michaels nodded and held a hand up. "I know that," he said. "But after what we saw this afternoon, I'm convinced there's more to this story than just one talented sixth grade tennis player."

"But, Dad, you already knew that," Jeff said. "You called Tom Ross and he said this went on all the time."

"I know it, Jeff," his father answered. "But that was sort of abstract. 'There are more out there,' is meaningless unless you actually find more out there. I think, rather than just ask Andi to go on-air and talk about what she's been dealing with this spring, it's time to start looking for those others who are out there."

At that point, Coach Dunphy chimed in. "When I was a very young coach, working at Penn as an assistant, I heard stories all the time about street agents and 'uncles' who had taken control of kids' lives when they were fourteen or fifteen—occasionally even younger.

"I didn't really believe it. Then, even though I was coaching at one of the best academic schools in the country, I came face-to-face with it over and over. You'd go to a summer camp or to an AAU Tournament and you'd be told if you wanted to talk to a kid you needed to deal with the AAU coach—who almost always had his hand out—or a so-called uncle or just a 'friend,' who was looking out for the kid. The parents and the high school coach often had nothing to do with it—although there were plenty of parents with their hands out, too."

Jeff had heard stories like that from his dad and had often read about that sort of thing, so he was certain Coach Dunphy wasn't exaggerating. Still . . .

"Coach, at least those kids were in high school, they were teenagers," he said. "Andi's eleven."

"True, but she's in a sport where players, especially girls, turn pro in their early teens and make a lot of money for doing so. I'm a tennis fan, so I follow this stuff closely. Jennifer Capriati turned pro at thirteen and was out of the sport for a good long while by eighteen. Coco Gauff was fifteen when she exploded onto the scene at Wimbledon in 2019 and within a year was talking about dealing with depression.

"And, by the way, those are the success stories. For every Capriati or Gauff who *do* make millions by turning pro young, there are hundreds, even thousands, who are pushed by parents or these agents—or as they like to say, 'non-agents'—to chase the money, but in the end aren't good enough. They get discarded along the way and we never hear about them. But their lives go on and are often very difficult. Same thing happens to those basketball phenoms who are surrounded by hangers-on and agents when they're kids but when they don't pan out as stars, they look around at some point and say, 'Where'd everybody go?'"

The group was silent for a moment as their waiter, who Tom Michaels had greeted as Joe when he walked up to the table, delivered drinks: beer for the adults, Cokes for the kids. Some bread came along, too. Hot and fresh.

"Okay then," Andi said finally. "If all this is true, what do you do next, Mr. Michaels? I really don't want another story on NBC Sports–Philly that's about me."

"First thing I have to do is talk to tennis coaches in the area about their best players—especially the girls because these guys go after them younger than boys."

"No boys at this age?" Jeff asked.

His dad shook his head. "No. Girls develop physically

faster than boys almost all the time—especially when it comes to sports. Every once in a while, a boy will turn pro at seventeen, but almost never before then."

"Wasn't Chang sixteen?" Coach Dunphy said, referring, Jeff knew, to Michael Chang.

"Yeah, he was," Jeff's dad said. "But he was an outlier. Played a different game than most men—all defense and running balls down, wearing guys out. He was also the youngest man to ever win a Slam when he won the French Open in 1989."

"How old was he?" Andi asked.

"Seventeen," Coach Dunphy said. "Interestingly, he never won another major."

"I'm not saying I won't check to see if there are any boys being pursued like this," Tom Michaels said. "I'm just guessing I'm going to find a lot more girls dealing with this than boys. If I'm wrong, that's fine."

Appetizers arrived. All three males had ordered massive shrimp cocktails. Andi had asked for lobster bisque.

"So, what's next then?" she asked.

"Two things—one that's up to me, one that's up to you," Tom Michaels said. "I need you to let the agents, non-agents, whatever they want to call themselves, make their pitches to you. Act as if you and your parents have given it some thought and at least want to hear what they have to say."

Andi made a face. Mr. Michaels nodded. "I get it, Andi," he said. "But information is power. We need as much information on these guys and from these guys as we can get."

"And what are you going to do, Dad?" Jeff asked.

"I'm going to start calling junior high school and high school coaches all over the area—suburbs, even into Delaware. I'm going to check the twelve-and-under and fourteen-and-under national rankings and call their coaches. There's no doubt in my mind I'll find others getting this sort of attention."

"You might find some liking it," Jeff said.

"I'm sure I will. And they may be the ones who are most willing to talk. This is the kind of reporting we used to do all the time when I worked for the *Daily News*; even when I first went to work for the TV station. Not anymore. I'll have to work on this on my off hours, and I'm not going to tell a soul until and unless we've got something. Andi, you willing to help?"

Andi sighed. "Yes, I guess so. I do think these people should be exposed for who they are."

"Any way I can help?" Jeff asked.

"Absolutely," Tom Michaels said. "Absolutely."

He dug into the shrimp cocktail.

17

JEFF'S NEW ASSIGNMENT WAS TO GET IN TOUCH WITH
Stevie Thomas, the kid reporter who was a freshman
at Penn and had written about him and Andi during
both soccer and basketball seasons.

"We need numbers to attack this project," Jeff's dad
explained to him on the drive home. "We need to check
a lot of places to find players who might have agents
chasing them. Some will be easy to find—because
they're ranked either nationally or in the East. Others
we're going to have to dig out—if they're there, which
I think they are."

"But why Stevie?"

Tom Michaels laughed. "Because he's a terrific
reporter; you can learn from him about journalism and
because he owes it to Andi to help because she talked

to him during basketball when she wasn't talking to other print reporters."

Jeff liked Stevie Thomas—although he was a little bit jealous of him. In many ways, Steve was who Jeff someday hoped to be: He had become a star in journalism at the age of thirteen when he had helped expose a plot to fix the national championship game in college basketball. His girlfriend—and frequent reporting partner—was Susan Carol Anderson, who had won three Olympic medals in swimming—two silver in butterfly and a gold in a relay. She was also tall, beautiful, and, as Stevie often pointed out, smarter than he was and now a freshman at Duke.

That night, Jeff texted Stevie and said he had a story that Stevie might want to pursue and asked if they could get together that weekend. Stevie texted back almost instantly.

Sure. Time? Place?

Jeff decided that the King of Prussia mall for lunch was a good idea. Thinking something besides pizza might be the right call, he suggested the Philly cheesesteak place. Having Andi there to fill in with some of her firsthand experiences would help considerably. When he suggested that, Steve wrote back with a thumbs-up and added, *Even if there's no story, getting a good cheesesteak will make the trip worth it.* At least, Jeff thought, he'd gotten one call right.

The good news was that Jeff was so fired up about being involved in chasing the story that he almost forgot about his frustrations with playing number two.

Almost.

On Friday, Villanova Middle School came to Merion to wrap up the first half of the season and the first half of the double round-robin. Merion would begin the second half of the season on Tuesday at Main Line, having beaten the One Kids (the Main Line was located on Route 1) at home to start the season.

Villanova was the only other unbeaten team in the conference. Jeff and Andi had read about their number one players in a story Andi had discovered in the *Philadelphia Inquirer*. They were twins, both thirteen and both were going to transfer to the IMG Academy in Florida when they started high school in the fall.

IMG Academy was a jock boarding school. Once, it had been a tennis academy, started by a tennis coach named Nick Bollettieri, who had coached—among others—major champions Andre Agassi and Jim Courier. IMG—the largest and richest sports agency in the world—had bought Bollettieri out in 1987 and had gradually expanded the academy to include basketball, golf, football, soccer, and track and field. It had changed its name to IMG Academy in 2002 and fielded nationally ranked teams in almost every sport.

The total cost to send a child to IMG Academy was about $70,000—the school's big selling point being that most of its graduates went to college on athletic scholarships. Of course, paying for *high school* pretty much wiped out the gains from going to college for free. Then again, true stars were often granted scholarships by IMG.

According to the *Inquirer* story, Tyler and Terri Porter were considered can't miss future stars and would only be paying "a fraction," of the normal tuition.

Jeff had groaned and put the story down when he got to a quote from their father saying that he thought IMG was, "the perfect place for aspiring student-athletes." His father had taught him long ago that if anyone used the term *student-athlete* there was no reason to believe another word they said.

"It's hypocritical," he had explained. "It's used to try to convince you that athletes really want to star in chemistry class. Or history. Which is very rarely the case. They want to be professional athletes. There's nothing wrong with that; just don't try to convince me they're choosing a college or, for that matter, a high school because of the quality of the English faculty.

The Porter twins were both tall: Tyler was about six foot two and Terri looked about five foot eleven.

She towered over Andi when they shook hands before the match. Andi knew her a little because they'd been at junior tournaments together although they'd never played one another since they were in different age groups.

For once, Jeff wasn't that upset about playing number two. Even playing one court over from where Tyler Porter and Gary Morrissey were playing, he could see that Gary was getting buried.

Jeff had his hands full playing Villanova's number two boy, Ricky Bowman. He wasn't nearly as intimidating as Porter, but he could play. In fact, his game was similar to Jeff's: His serve was decent, but not dominant; his ground strokes were solid, and he rarely ventured to the net. Jeff won the first set in a tiebreak and was down 1–2 in the second when he noticed Tyler Porter and Gary Morrissey shaking hands. He glanced at the mini-scoreboard under the umpire's chair and saw that Gary had lost 6–1, 6–2.

He was standing to walk back onto the court when he heard a ruckus coming from that court. He and Bowman both stopped to see what was going on. Gary was long gone—nowhere in sight. There was a man in front of Porter, screaming at him as his son pulled on his sweater.

Even at a distance, Jeff could hear him clearly. "Three games! You lost three games! What is wrong with you? I'm not spending all this money on you to watch you lose three games to a kid you should beat playing left-handed!"

Jeff saw one of the Villanova coaches come in to get the man—who he assumed was Porter's father—away from his son.

He and Bowman were standing at their respective service lines. Jeff glanced at Bowman, who shrugged and said, "He's worse with the daughter."

Maybe the embarrassing scene took something out of Bowman. He wasn't the same player after that. Jeff won the second set 6–4. When they shook hands, Bowman smiled and said, "Good thing you didn't play Tyler. You might have won *four* games and then his dad would have really gone ballistic."

The number one girls' match had now drawn a crowd. With the team 5–0 and word of Andi's prowess having spread around the school, a decent crowd had showed up to watch the match—even without knowing about the Porter twins.

Jeff walked over to join the crowd. He could see that the girls had split the first two sets and were at 2–all in the third set. There wasn't a lot of finesse to Terri Porter's game. She played serve and volley—rushing to the net after each serve to try for an unhittable volley of Andi's return. Still, Andi's speed and the consistency of her ground strokes were clearly giving her trouble.

"She completely overwhelmed Andi the first set," Coach O'Grady told him after Andi had held to lead 3–2. "I doubt Andi has ever faced that sort of power or that type of game. But she's adapted. I think she's got her on her heels a little bit now."

Jeff noticed Porter's dad, her brother, Tyler, and the Villanova coach standing not too far from the chair where Terri Porter was sitting during the changeover.

"Papa bear trying to give instructions?" Jeff asked.

Coach O'Grady laughed.

"Soon as he got through yelling at the son, they walked over there with the coach right behind, no doubt to try and keep an eye on him."

Parents were not allowed to coach their kids during matches—with good reason. The last thing any kid needed was having an overbearing parent—like Porter Senior—telling them what to do or berating them. If they needed coaching, that's what the coaches were there for.

Terri Porter might have been reeling a bit, but she still had a serve that was almost impossible to break. On a couple of occasions, she spun second serves that bounced so high Andi had to literally reach straight up to get her racquet on the ball.

They stayed on serve until 5–all when Andi, looking just a little bit tired, served a double fault to go down a break point. Jeff was sweating profusely by now, even though it was a cool afternoon and he'd been off the court for more than half an hour.

Andi walked around in a circle for a moment behind the baseline and Jeff could see she was talking to herself. He'd never seen that before.

Her first serve on the break point was a second serve—instead of going for straight power, she spun the ball wide and then, no doubt surprising Porter, she charged the net. Porter was off-balance and her return floated. Andi pounced on it and slammed a forehand volley into the open court.

Break point saved. Jeff breathed a sigh of relief.

Andi didn't often talk to herself on the tennis court. But when she double-faulted to go down break point, she decided she needed a talking to—so she gave herself one.

"You are *not* losing to this girl," she said under her breath. "She can serve, and she can volley, but her ground strokes suck." She smiled for a split second because she knew her parents would not be happy to hear her use that word—even when no one could hear her.

She took a deep breath and decided to catch Porter off-balance with a second serve. It worked. Two more good serves and she was out of the game, up 6–5.

Walking to sit down during the changeover, she could see that the other singles matches were finished, and her teammates and the Villanova singles players were all gathered behind the court. With her peripheral vision, she had tracked the other matches and was pretty certain Villanova was up 3–2, meaning Merion had to have her match.

She decided she needed something different to try to break Porter's serve. She didn't want the match to come down to a tiebreak. There was too much luck involved in a tiebreak.

At times, she had tried standing way back to receive serve to give her more time to line up her returns against Porter's power. It had worked occasionally, but not enough. She decided to try something completely different and stood inside the baseline as Porter lined up her first serve.

She could see the look of surprise on Porter's face. She bounced the ball a couple of extra times and then served the ball so hard and so high that it almost hit Andi in the face, whizzing past her after bouncing well beyond the service line. Porter grimaced. Her second serve spun right to Andi's forehand and she cracked it into the corner. Porter ran it down, but her down-the-line backhand went wide.

At love–15, Porter took something off her first serve in order to make sure she got it in, figuring Andi would have trouble handling it. Andi took it early and chipped it to Porter's feet. One thing about being tall was that getting to low balls was often difficult. Porter's scooped half-volley hit the net tape.

It was love–30. Now it was Porter's turn to take a walk before serving. Both girls were hearing yells of encouragement from their teammates.

Porter went back to blasting her first serve. This time she nailed it and the ball whizzed past Andi. It was 15–30.

Porter tried another blast. Andi took a step back, fought off the high hop and hit the return directly at Porter, who had followed the serve to net. It was sheer luck that the ball went into Porter's body. She tried to fight it off, but her volley barely cleared the net. Andi closed and easily put it away.

Suddenly, shockingly, it was match point: 15–40.

Andi decided to make Porter wait in the hot seat. She walked quickly to her chair and toweled off for a moment. Porter was practically twitching when Andi walked back to take her position just inside the baseline.

"That's a delay! Call it, Terri!" a voice bellowed. Terri Porter had to hear the voice, but she ignored it. She served another bullet—it was long. Andi crept closer to the service line. To her surprise, Porter unleashed another first serve—no spin, just power.

It was also long—clearly long. Andi pointed a finger in the air to indicate the serve was long. Game, set, match. Porter's shoulders sagged as she jogged to the net.

"That ball was in!" came the same bellowing voice. "The girl's hooking! Serve was good!" *Hooking* was the tennis word for cheating.

Before Andi could turn in the direction of the voice to say, "Are you nuts, it wasn't close!" Terri Porter turned to the voice.

"Dad, the ball was long. I could tell from here. Stop it!"

She continued to the net, shook hands and said, "I'm sorry about that. My dad is a little bit intense."

Andi reached up to put an arm around Terri's shoulders. "Don't worry about it," she said. "That was a great match." Then she added, "Don't let him bother you," figuring that was pretty close to impossible. How do you ignore your father?

The two girls walked to their waiting teammates. Andi accepted the congratulations and then said, "What's the score?"

Coach Foster answered. "You just made it 3–3. We're winning one doubles and losing the others. You need to get some water and some rest because it looks like you're going to be playing mixed doubles in a few minutes."

That was fine with Andi. She was tired, but she knew a few minutes of rest and adrenaline would carry her. She assumed the Porter twins would be the opposition.

"Who am I playing with if we have to play?" she asked.

Coach Foster gave her a funny look. "Gary," he said. "He's our number one boy. Who else would you play with?"

Andi didn't answer. She wasn't looking at either coach. She was looking at Jeff, who had turned and walked away.

18

AS IT TURNED OUT, AS COACH FOSTER HAD PREDICTED, THE doubles matches were split. That meant mixed doubles would decide the match. The coaches agreed to take a ten-minute break to give Andi and Terri Porter a few extra minutes to cool off. Andi knew Jeff needed cooling off a lot more than she did. He had walked to a bench on the far side of the court and was sitting by himself.

"I understand why you're disappointed," she said.

"I'm *not* disappointed," he said. "I'm angry. Are they even *watching*? I'll bet if they asked Gary who should play, he'd say me."

"You want to know what I think?" she said. "Tell me, because if you don't want to know what I think, I'll just walk away because if you're going to snap at me, I'll pass."

He turned and looked at her. She was standing there, racquet in hand, ready to go and play again.

"Okay," he said. "What do you think?"

"I think the coaches believe judging Gary on today's match isn't fair because that Porter kid is really good," she said. "And I think they believe Gary should play mixed again because we won easily the last time we played together."

"You think you're going to win easily today?" he said.

"No, I don't, but—"

She was interrupted by Coach O'Grady's voice, coming from the other side of the courts. "Come on, Andi, time to go," she said, urgency in her voice.

Andi started to say something, but Jeff held a hand up: "Go," he said. "Go play."

"We'll talk later," she said, turning to jog back to where everyone from both teams was gathering.

Jeff decided he'd stay and sulk alone. The four players went on court a minute later for a quick warm-up. At that point, Jeff heard Coach Foster's voice cutting sharply through the air: "Jeff Michaels," he said, "you part of this team or not?"

Jeff slowly stood up and walked back to where everyone else was standing. When he got there, Coach Foster greeted him. "I know you're disappointed you aren't playing," he said. "Coach O'Grady and I understand. But we expect you to support your team-mates, regardless."

When Jeff didn't respond, Coach Foster said: "Did you hear me?"

"Yes, Coach, I did."

He honestly didn't know how he felt as the match started. He could never root against Andi, but if she and Gary won it would only solidify the coaches' belief that they had made the right decision. He clapped when Andi or Gary hit a winner and joined the others in shouting encouragement. But his heart wasn't in it.

In the end, it didn't really matter. Andi and Terri Porter were about as evenly matched as doubles play-ers as they had been playing singles. But the gap between Tyler Porter and Gary Morrissey was notice-able. Neither Merion player had much chance against Porter's serve and Gary had little chance against Terri Porter's serve, not having the benefit of facing it for three sets the way Andi had.

Andi held serve twice. Those were the only two games Merion won. Villanova won the set, 8–2, and the rest of the team piled onto the court to celebrate as soon as the handshakes were over. A step behind them was Mr. Porter, high-fiving as if he was part of the team. He then walked over to Gary and Andi and put out a hand.

As Andi reluctantly shook it, he said, "I'm sorry

I accused you of hooking during the singles match. I get a little bit caught up in the emotions of the matches."

As luck would have it, Jeff was right behind Porter Senior and heard what he said.

"Ya think?" he said.

Porter turned to see where the words had come from. Seeing Jeff, he smiled. "I'm trying to be a good sport here and you're giving me a hard time?"

"Easy to be a good sport when you win," Jeff said.

Porter was glaring at him. "What kind of a rude punk are you?" he said. "What's your problem?"

Jeff wasn't about to back down, even though he was giving away about eight inches and, he guessed, close to a hundred pounds to the twins' father. He took a step toward him, but before he could get close enough for anything to happen, Coach Foster and Andi had stepped between them.

"I'm sorry, Mr. Porter. Jeff's a little upset because this is our first loss," Coach Foster said. "Jeff, please tell Mr. Porter you're sorry for speaking to him that way."

Jeff's first instinct was to say, "No way," but Andi, who had put her hands on his shoulders to move him backward, whispered, "Just do it."

"I'm sorry," Jeff said. He shook loose from Andi and walked away. He wasn't going to deal with Coach

Foster telling him the apology was inadequate—even though he knew it was.

Coach O'Grady was waving everyone over for the post-match cheer. Slowly, he walked over to join the rest of the team. She waited for him. They did the cheer.

Jeff went and found his racquet and pulled his phone out of his racquet case. His dad was working a Flyers playoff game that night and his mom had told him to call as soon as the match was over. That would give her time to get to the school while he showered. Now, he wished he'd called before the mixed doubles started so he could go straight to the car and get out of there.

As he finished his text, he turned and saw Terri Porter standing there. He felt as if he was standing in a hole because she was at least four or five inches taller than he was. Still, he couldn't help but notice how pretty she was, especially after taking her cap off and letting her long, brown hair down.

"I just wanted to tell you I'm sorry about my dad," she said. "I already apologized to Andi. It's not so bad when he yells at Tyler and me, we're used to it. But it's not fair when he lets his emotions affect the way he treats other kids."

Jeff smiled, very relieved at that moment to have parents who were supportive, but not crazy or domineering.

"Thanks," he said. "No worries. I know it wasn't your fault or your brother's fault. But I appreciate you saying that. By the way, you guys are both really good."

"I'm not as good as Andi and she's two years younger than I am," Terri said. "She's a real star."

Jeff nodded. "Yeah, but you two are very good."

"Just good enough to have a father who makes our lives miserable."

Someone was calling her name. "Come on, Terri, we're going."

She held her hand up and Jeff gave her a high five. "Well, guess we'll see you again in a few weeks. Good luck," she said.

"Good luck to you, too," Jeff said. He meant it—but he wasn't talking about tennis. He'd forgotten about feeling sorry for himself. At that moment, he felt sorry for the Porter twins.

19

STEVIE THOMAS WAS WAITING AT AN EMPTY TABLE THE NEXT morning when Andi and Jeff showed up, having been dropped off at the mall by Andi's father.

If Jeff was a little bit jealous of Stevie, Andi was just a tad jealous of his girlfriend, Susan Carol Anderson. Or, at the very least, she occasionally fantasized about growing up to be like her.

It wasn't Susan Carol's appearance. Andi was already five foot seven and she was very secure about her looks. It was more about what Susan Carol had accomplished: three Olympic medals at the age of fifteen, an academic scholarship to Duke, not to mention her journalism career. At eighteen, she had already accomplished more than most reporters would accomplish in a lifetime. And Andi knew from reading some of the countless stories that had been written about her, she had no interest in using her looks to get a job in television. She'd already had plenty of offers.

"Being on television isn't being a reporter," she'd been quoted as saying in one story. "I did it for a little while, so I know that firsthand. I want to be a great reporter someday. That's my goal: not being on TV because someone thinks I look good in a short skirt and high heels."

The only part of that statement that Andi disputed was the part about being a great reporter *someday*. Susan Carol was already a great reporter.

So was Stevie Thomas. He'd treated Andi very fairly during the two media frenzies she'd already been caught up in—the controversy over her being denied a spot on the soccer team because the coach wanted an all-boys team and then the revolt she'd help lead to have the coach removed during basketball season. That had become a big story in Philadelphia when Jeff and his dad convinced Fran Dunphy, a Philly icon, to become the team's coach for the final games of the season.

Now it was Andi who needed Stevie, not the other way around when he had wanted her to talk to him and give him insights she hadn't given to TV reporters.

It was a good sign that he had arrived early. Andi

and Jeff walked into the food court at 11:28—two minutes early—and Stevie was already there. They all shook hands and agreed the first order of business was to head to the cheesesteak counter before the place got crowded.

They took their drinks to the table while they waited for their food. Andi and Stevie had ordered traditional cheesesteaks—which were considered a delicacy in most of Philadelphia. Jeff ordered his without cheese, causing Stevie to give him a look.

"I know you love pizza," he said. "So why do you like cheese on pizza, but not on a Philly cheesesteak?"

"Actually, the reason I like Andy's so much is they go light on the cheese," he said. "I can tolerate it that way. But on steak? No thanks."

"So, to what do I owe this honor?" Stevie said as they sat down.

"We have a story for you," Andi said. "But it won't be easy to get."

"Those are the best stories," Stevie said. "There's usually a reason why a story is easy—because there's not much to it. Why don't you start at the beginning?"

Andi did just that. When she began to talk about her rankings, in the East and nationally, Stevie broke in for a second. "So, you're telling me you're *better* at tennis than basketball or soccer? Seriously?"

Andi dropped her head at that moment, a little bit

embarrassed. Jeff jumped in. "Trust me, she's a lot better in tennis than soccer or basketball."

Stevie smiled. "I just broke rule one of reporting: Never interrupt someone mid-story. Sorry. Go on, Andi."

Andi did, telling him about the ambush meetings staged by Tad Walters, Pete Singer—including the one on Jeff—and Renee Stubing. Plus, her father's conversation with Tom Ross, who had worked as a tennis agent forever.

Stevie didn't interrupt again.

"So, you want me to talk to some of these agents to find out how far they'll go to try to get your name on a contract?" he said. "I can answer that one for you—very far."

"No," Andi said, shaking her head. "I don't want this story to be about me."

For once, Stevie Thomas looked puzzled. "But the story *is* about you," he said. "You and the dirtbag agents."

Andi shook her head again. "I'm a small part of the story—the real story," she said. "Tom Ross told my dad this goes on all the time in tennis. Has gone on for years. I'll bet you anything those twins we played against yesterday have an agent involved in their life. And their dad is probably okay with it."

"I'll bet there are a dozen kids just in the Philly area

who aren't even in high school yet who either have an agent or have agents pursuing them," Jeff added. "My dad's going to work the story, too, using his contacts to try to find the right kids." He paused and said, "or the wrong kids, depending on your point of view."

"So, I'd be competing with your dad for the story?" Stevie said.

"No," Jeff said. "I think he looks at this and we look at this as something to work on together. If we get the story, work it out so both the newspaper and the TV station break it together." He hesitated and then added: "There's also the possibility that the TV station won't want the story. It's not Eagles, Phillies, Flyers, or Sixers. That's about all they care about these days."

They heard the name "Andi," being called, meaning their sandwiches were ready.

As they walked up to claim the food and get soda refills, Stevie commented: "I hate to say it, but your dad might be right about the TV people not wanting it even if it's there. Local TV these days and even network TV is only about the major sports and celebrities. Your dad's station barely even covers college basketball anymore and we're living in the best college basketball city in the country."

"I know," Jeff said, checking his sandwich to make sure it didn't have any cheese on it. Andi had gotten soda refills and she handed Stevie his drink and took a sandwich, once Jeff had claimed the one with no cheese.

"Whether the TV station is interested or not is something for us to worry about later," she said once they were reseated. "First, we worry about getting the story. Then we figure out what to do with it."

Stevie and Jeff both nodded, each happy they didn't have to pause in order to talk.

By the time the food had been devoured and the trays lay completely empty, they had put together a game plan.

Tom Michaels would work local coaches. He had a lot of contacts at the high school level, mostly in football and basketball, but Jeff was certain they could put him in touch with tennis coaches. The high school coaches at that level could lead him to coaches who had stars on their middle school teams.

Stevie would start with the Porter twins, who, Andi and Jeff were convinced, would willingly talk to him— if not on the record, then on background to give him guidance and tell him about other kids who were being recruited by agents and by IMG Academy. Perhaps there was a connection?

"At the very least you need to find out who their father's been in contact with," Andi said. "I have a feeling the kids have had very little say in any of this."

Stevie was taking notes. "I'm fine with this, but I really think one of you should be there when I try to talk to these guys," he said. "They're a lot more apt to talk if they think they're dealing with a peer— especially another tennis player."

"Andi should do it," Jeff said. "She's the one being recruited."

"Yeah, but I think she kind of liked you," Andi said. "She was the one who went out of her way to talk to you after the match yesterday."

Jeff felt himself redden a little. He hadn't realized that Andi had even noticed the conversation.

"Come on," he said. "She's a foot taller than I am and way out of my league. She was just being nice about the way her father behaved. She and Tyler probably end up doing that a lot."

At that moment, Andi felt a slight twinge, one she didn't recognize right away. Could it be possible that she was bothered by Jeff referring to another girl as "way out of his league"? It wasn't so much that she thought Jeff had any serious interest in Terri Porter, it was just the notion that he actually noticed other girls. That bothered her, at least a little bit.

She realized Stevie and Jeff were both looking at her, waiting for some kind of response.

"You get it set up, Stevie, and then we'll see what we can work out in terms of time and place to meet with them."

In the meantime, Jeff would try to find out who else in the Philadelphia area might be a candidate to be pursued by the agents. Stevie gave him the name of a reporter at the *Inquirer/Daily News* who covered high school sports. "There's a decent chance, I'd think, that she knows who some of the up-and-comers are in tennis in the area," he said. "She writes about high school tennis a fair bit in the spring. She might even have access to more direct information than your father will through the coaches."

Stevie leaned back in his seat. "I swear I could eat another steak sandwich," he said. "But I'll regret it an hour from now."

Jeff understood. He felt the same way. Andi stood up. "Time for us to get to work then, right?" she said. "Stevie, let us know when you make contact with the Porter twins."

Stevie stood up and gave her a mock salute. "I'm used to taking orders," he said. "I've worked with Susan Carol for a long time. I'm on it."

20

JEFF SPENT SUNDAY AT HOME, CATCHING UP ON SOME homework and watching the Phillies early in the afternoon and then a golf tournament from Hilton Head in the late afternoon.

Stevie emailed him midafternoon to say that he was going to Villanova's match against Haverford on Tuesday and hoped to talk to at least one of the Porter kids there. "The father can't be with both of them all the time," he wrote. "If he wants to know who I am, I'll tell him the truth—that I'm a reporter interested in writing about his kids. My guess is he'll love that."

It was good thinking. Jeff's read of Mr. Porter was the same as Stevie's: The only thing the guy *might* like more than his kids making him rich was his kids making him famous.

He spent the rest of the day in front of the television,

his mind drifting off to what he should do about his own situation on the tennis team. He really didn't want to consult with his parents or even Andi anymore. He decided his choice was simple: just accept what was going on or go to the coaches and ask them why they continued to insist on keeping the lineup the same.

In truth, things weren't that bad. It wasn't as if this was soccer season, and he wasn't getting to play very much at all. He had a 6–0 record in singles and felt as if the competition had forced him to improve his game. He was looking forward to playing tournaments in the summer to see how far he'd come since last year.

The flip side was that he honestly believed he should be back playing number one *and* being Andi's partner when mixed doubles had to be played to decide a match. If he was being honest with himself, it was the mixed doubles part of the equation that bothered him the most. If he'd been playing number one singles all along, he knew he wouldn't be undefeated; he would probably have lost twice.

But he was convinced he and Andi might have beaten the Porter twins and won the match for Merion against Villanova. Not a lock, that was certain, but he would have liked to have had the chance. Jeff was, if nothing else, intensely competitive. He wanted to be part of a decisive match, and he especially wanted to be part of a decisive match with Andi as his partner.

Beyond all of that, he really wanted to know why the coaches had treated him this way. He didn't think it was personal—he'd never had any sort of hostile interaction with either as part of the team, and they both taught eighth grade, so he'd never encountered them in the classroom.

So then, why? Why had they dropped him from number one when he hadn't lost a match? The only other person who had been dropped from a spot was Mindy Garceau and *she lost* a match and was clearly better suited to play doubles. That made sense.

He could even understand experimenting by having him switch spots with Gary Morrissey. Jeff knew if they played ten matches, they'd probably both win five times. So, switch them for a match—maybe two. But Gary was 2–2 playing at number one and could easily be 1–3. Making it worse was the coaches use of the logic that the number ones should play mixed doubles together, regardless of who seemed to be playing better—or at the very least having more success—in the singles.

As Rory McIlroy was walking up the eighteenth fairway on his TV set en route to winning the golf tournament, Jeff made a decision. He would go and talk to the coaches. But how would he set it up? Who did he contact first? Would they even agree to meet with him? The thought of asking his dad, who was now sitting next to him watching McIlroy, crossed his mind. He decided against it, if only because he thought his dad might try to talk him out of it. His mind was made up. His gut told him this was the right thing to do.

He waited until McIlroy drained one last birdie putt and did the winner's required post-round interview. He wasn't sure why he bothered to watch, they were all the same—except, he had to admit, on occasion with McIlroy. He had this tendency to tell the truth, which often got him criticized by the golf media. His dad always said, "You go beyond birdies and bogeys with most of these media guys, they get confused. It's why they like Tiger Woods so much. He never says anything."

He picked up his phone and sent a joint text to his coaches. Everyone on the team had their cell numbers. He wrote slowly, choosing his words carefully: *Coach Foster/Coach O'Grady* (he even took time deciding which coach's name to put first, deciding finally to make it alphabetical)*: I'm writing to ask if you might have a few moments to talk to me tomorrow at school. I could meet you in one of your classrooms during lunch or somewhere that is convenient for you before we start practice. I'll only need a few minutes of your time. Thanks so much . . . Respectfully, Jeff Michaels.*

There was no response before dinner. When dinner was over, Jeff went upstairs to his room to check on emails. Walking up the steps he glanced at his phone and saw there was a text from Coach Foster: *Come to my classroom—304—at the start of the lunch period tomorrow. Coach O'Grady and I will meet you there.*

It wasn't exactly filled with warmth, but they had accepted his request. Now, all he had to do was figure out exactly what he wanted to say and how he wanted to say it.

Since he knew he wouldn't be at lunch on time, Jeff sent Andi an early morning text to let her know he was going to see Coach Foster and Coach O'Grady at the start of lunch, so he'd be a little late.

Her response was brief: *You sure about this?*

His response was briefer: *Yes.*

He didn't hear much that was being said during his morning classes. He was going over what he wanted to say again and again. At one point he reminded himself that he wasn't writing the Gettysburg Address, that he needed to get to the point quickly and not ramble. And then he remembered that the Gettysburg Address was only 272 words long and it had taken Abraham Lincoln under four minutes to deliver it.

So maybe he should be thinking about the Gettysburg Address.

When the fourth-period bell finally rang, he bolted

for the door. Then he realized he didn't want to rush, and he didn't want anyone to *see* him rushing to the stairs and up to the third floor. So, he deliberately slowed his pace.

He arrived at room 304 at the same time as Coach O'Grady. They exchanged awkward greetings and walked inside. Coach Foster was sitting at his desk. It appeared that he was grading papers.

"Joan, Jeff, come on in," he said.

He stood up, rolled his chair around the desk and said, "Let's all of us grab chairs and talk." He nodded in the direction of two chairs that weren't attached to writing desks. They all sat. "Jeff, I'm pretty sure Coach O'Grady and I know what this is about, but why don't you go ahead and tell us and we can go from there?"

Jeff nodded. For a moment he was distracted deciding whether to keep both feet on the floor or cross his legs to look more casual. He decided to keep his feet on the floor. There was nothing casual about this meeting—certainly not as far as he was concerned.

"First, thank you both for taking the time to meet with me," he said. "I know this is the one time all day you get a chance to catch your breath."

"And to eat," Coach O'Grady said with a smile to let Jeff know she wasn't complaining.

"Right," he said. "Me too."

Her comment distracted him for a moment from his

prepared speech. He took a deep breath to stall and regroup mentally.

"What I wanted, really, is to ask if you could explain to me why I got dropped from number one to number two when no one else has been dropped anywhere in the lineup except after a loss?" He held up a hand when Coach Foster started to say something. "Sorry, Coach, can I finish please? I don't mean to be rude but . . ."

"I understand, Jeff, my bad," Coach Foster said. "Go ahead."

"Anyway, like I said, I got the notion of experimenting a little when you did it since Gary and I are pretty evenly matched, but since then, he's struggled in every match and I'm still unbeaten and twice you played him with Andi in mixed doubles even though I'm pretty sure I was playing better that day."

All of that came in a rush, in part to get it out, in part because of nerves.

The two coaches looked at each other as if deciding who should respond. It was Coach Foster who finally spoke.

"Let me say first, Jeff, that you're absolutely entitled to ask these questions," he said. "And, you guessed right, when we switched you and Gary it was just to see how it went. The truth is, it's gone very well. You've won a couple matches at number two that Gary might not have won and the matches he's lost, well, we both think you'd probably have lost them, too."

Jeff knew they weren't wrong. He started to respond, but this time Coach Foster put up a hand. "We let you finish, Jeff, so how about you let me finish?"

"Of course, Coach. Sorry."

"The mixed doubles is a little more complicated—but not much. Right from the beginning, we've tried to do things as objectively as possible. The tryouts were based strictly on the results of the matches that were played, right? The original lineup was also put together based strictly on those results. So, when we got into a position where we had to make a decision on mixed doubles, we stayed objective and put our number one players together to play."

Jeff waited a moment to see if he was finished. He looked at Coach O'Grady to see if she wanted to add anything. She nodded at him to indicate it was his turn.

"But the one decision you made that was *not* objective was dropping me behind Gary," he said. "So just saying we went with the number one players because it was an objective decision isn't right because making Gary number one was *not* an objective decision. And keeping him there wasn't objective either."

For the first time Coach O'Grady spoke up. "He's pretty sharp for an eleven-year-old, Bill," she said.

Coach Foster nodded and smiled at Jeff. "So, what do you think we should do, Jeff?" he said. "What's fair?"

Jeff shrugged because the answer—to him—was pretty clear.

"Put me back at number one tomorrow," he said. "And, if we have to play mixed doubles, give me a crack at playing with Andi. I'll bet Gary won't object."

Now both coaches smiled—but they weren't happy smiles. In fact, they were more like grimaces.

"You're right," Coach Foster finally said. "In fact, I think Gary might be relieved to not have to play number one. But his father wouldn't be very happy about it. In fact, he'd be downright unhappy."

Jeff was baffled. "His father?" he said. "Who's his father?"

Coach O'Grady shrugged. "You're bound to find out at some point so we might as well tell you," she said. "He's the president of Aces Inc." She paused and then added, "I'm sorry, Jeff. I let you down. This is my fault."

21

IT TOOK JEFF A MOMENT TO REMEMBER WHERE HE'D HEARD the name Aces Inc. before. Then it came to him: Andi had mentioned that she'd been told they were interested in her in much the same way that New Advantage and ProStyles were. They were the group that only represented tennis players. They were also the group that hadn't had someone show up to try to recruit Andi in person.

Now Jeff suspected he knew why.

Coach O'Grady had stood from her chair and was pacing around the room as if trying to decide what to say next. Jeff said nothing, remembering what his father had told him often about sometimes letting silence be the next question during an interview.

"Look, I never meant for you or anyone else to be treated unfairly or get hurt in any of this," she said.

"Tennis has been part of my life since I was a girl grow-ing up in Florida. I was one of those kids who was just good enough to get pushed into the sport by my parents but not quite good enough to really make it as a pro."

She paused for a moment, realized that neither Jeff nor Coach Foster was going to say anything and then, standing behind her chair, continued.

"I turned pro when I graduated from high school. I could have gone to the University of Florida to play, but an agent named Bobby Austin convinced me and my parents there was money to be made right away if I turned pro.

"He wasn't completely wrong. I got a couple of decent contracts—racquet deal, shoe deal, clothing deal—as soon as I turned pro. It was enough to pay my expenses for a couple of years. Fortunately, my parents were smart enough to sock some of the money away for me to go to college—in case I had to go at some point.

"I played the Futures tour for a couple of years and got nowhere."

For the first time Jeff interrupted. "Futures tour?" he asked.

"It's the minor league of women's tennis. You play well enough there, get your ranking high enough, you start to get into real tournaments playing for real money. I never got to that point. My highest ranking was 386. I did get to play in a couple of WTA tournaments in Florida because I got a wild card as a local kid.

"First time I played Elise Burgin, who was a real player, ranked in the 20s at some point. I won one game. Next time I played a teenage kid no one had heard of named Monica Seles. Guess what? I got one game off her, too. You gotta give me points for consistency."

When neither Jeff nor Coach Foster laughed at her attempt at humor, she plunged on.

"I was done after two years. The money I'd gotten starting out was gone and my ranking had actually gone *down*. I was a mess. I applied to Florida but, since I was no longer eligible to play tennis for them since I was a pro, they turned me down. I ended up getting into North Florida and was able to transfer to Florida after two years because I had good grades."

It was Coach Foster who spoke next. "Joan, all due respect, I think we all want to have time to eat. Can we cut to the chase?"

Coach O'Grady nodded. "Sorry, TMI, I guess."

Actually, Jeff had been fascinated by her story, but said nothing.

"I stayed involved on the fringes of tennis even after college and after I started teaching. I know a number of tennis coaches on the high school and college level and a handful who have coached pros. I've always counseled them not to push kids to turn pro unless they were absolutely, 100 percent sure-fire top fifty or better type players.

"I've *never* seen a kid who wasn't at least in high school who fit that description until I saw Andi."

"When was that?" Jeff asked.

"Last summer," she answered. "I run a number of junior tournaments for the Pennsylvania Tennis Association. You could see right away Andi was special. She was beating twelve-year-olds regularly, some of them very good twelve-year-olds who were bigger and stronger than she was.

"Gary played in several of those tournaments, too. For an eleven-year-old he did well, too, but nothing like Andi. I taught his older sister, Bridget, a couple years ago. She's a tenth grader now and never took to tennis, although not for lack of trying on her parents' part. I knew that Alex had started Aces Inc. a couple years ago and they'd had pretty good success.

"One evening we were watching Gary play and Alex asked if I'd have any interest in coming to work for him as a talent scout. He knew my background; knew I'd been around the game most of my life. The pay would be much more than I make teaching and I'd be back in tennis full time.

"I'd already committed to teaching this year and he was fine with that. In fact, he was very fine with that because he knew—not sure how, but he did—that Andi was coming to school here.

"'That's your first recruit,' he said. 'She's got absolute star potential.' To make a long story shorter, I knew he was right."

"Which is when you emailed me and asked if I had a co-coach yet?" Coach Foster asked, who was clearly hearing all or most of this for the first time.

Coach O'Grady nodded. "I thought it was a win-win for me," she said. "I knew I'd enjoy coaching the kids—and I have—but I also knew it was a way for me to get to know Andi without having to put any pressure on her like those other agents have been doing. And to be honest, it was going as well as I could possibly have hoped until Alex decided he wanted Gary to be number one *and* wanted to see him playing mixed doubles with Andi."

"Which is why you suggested we make the switch," said a now angry-looking Coach Foster.

"And it's why I've put you off when you wanted to switch Jeff and Gary back," she said. "And why I insisted Friday that Gary and Andi play the mixed even though it was obvious Jeff should play with her."

The fifteen-minute bell was ringing. Jeff had completely forgotten his hunger. He was stunned by what he'd just heard.

"I was afraid if I didn't do what Alex wanted me to

do, the job he'd promised me wouldn't be there at the end of the school year."

"So now what happens?" Jeff asked.

Coach O'Grady looked at Coach Foster. "I don't suppose moving Jeff back to number one for the Main Line match tomorrow would be enough?" she said.

"No," Coach Foster said, "I don't suppose it will be."

For some reason a ridiculous thought popped into Jeff's head at that moment. He wondered if Fran Dunphy knew much about tennis.

22

THERE WAS NO SIGN OF COACH O'GRADY AT PRACTICE THAT
afternoon. Jeff hadn't had a chance to tell anyone what
had happened, not even Andi, but he wasn't shocked.

Coach Foster addressed the team before they
started their warm-ups. "Everyone, I'm sorry to report
to you that Coach O'Grady is no longer going to be
one of your coaches," he said. "It turns out she had a
conflict of interest that will prevent her from coaching
here any longer. I'm hoping to find a replacement for
her from among the faculty, but don't know if that will
happen."

Andi was looking directly at Jeff, her eyes filled
with question marks. But she said nothing.

"Okay, let's everyone stretch and get warm," Coach
Foster said.

That wouldn't be too tough, the temperature was in

the 80s, hot for a mid-April day. Jeff warmed up with Gary Morrissey.

"What do you think that's all about?" Gary asked as they stood near the net hitting volleys at each other.

It had never occurred to Jeff that Gary wouldn't know. Now, he realized there was really no reason for him to know. Just the opposite in fact: His dad wouldn't want him to be aware that he was only playing number one because of his dad's influence.

Not to mention the Andi business.

Jeff couldn't feign ignorance because he knew the whole story was going to come out. But he had no desire to be the one to deliver the news to Gary: "Hey, did you know your dad is a sleaze who is trying to get to Andi just like a bunch of other sleazy agents?"

No thanks.

As soon as Jeff turned on his phone at the end of practice there was a text from Andi—he wasn't surprised, just amazed how quickly she'd sent it to him.

When can we talk?

Jeff texted back that he'd call when he got home. He wanted to talk to his dad, who was picking him up, before he talked to Andi.

OK. But as SOON as you get home.

He sent back a thumbs-up.

He hadn't told his parents that he was going to meet with the coaches, so he had to fill his dad in on his request for the meeting and then what had happened.

"She just came out and admitted it?" his dad said when Jeff was finished. "I wonder why she'd do that?"

"Not sure, but I think she felt guilty about the whole thing," Jeff said. "I think she felt guilty about demoting me, but beyond that I think she felt pretty bad about stalking an eleven-year-old girl to try to get a job."

His dad nodded. "She should feel bad about that. I wonder if she feels bad enough to go on camera and talk about it. My guess is whatever career she thought she was going to have with Aces Inc. is pretty much out the window now."

Jeff hadn't really thought about that. For that matter, he hadn't even thought about whether Coach O'Grady's admission and departure would mean he'd be back to playing number one singles the next day.

As they turned into the driveway, a text popped into his phone. It was from Stevie Thomas: *Progress. Need to talk to you and Andi tonight.*

He read the text to his dad, who smiled.

"The plot gets thicker and thicker," he said as they pulled into the garage. "Call Andi first."

He needn't have said it. Jeff was punching her speed-dial number into the phone as they walked through the door.

There was a long silence on the other end of the phone after Jeff had taken Andi through the details of the lunchtime meeting. Jeff waited, knowing she needed a moment or two to digest what he'd just told her.

Finally, just before he was going to ask if she was still there, Andi said, "I actually thought she liked me."

"I'm sure she does like you," Jeff said, hearing some hurt in her voice. "But she clearly was hoping to use you to get the job she wanted."

"That's not exactly the definition of a friend, is it?" she said.

No, it wasn't, he thought.

He changed the subject—slightly. "My dad thinks she might be willing to go on camera and talk about all this now that she's been outed."

"She outed herself," Andi said. "I'd like to know why she did that. She didn't have to. She could have just said, 'Let's put Jeff back at number one' and that would have been the end of it. Didn't you say she told you Coach Foster already wanted to do that?"

She had. Jeff agreed with Andi. There had to be a reason why Coach O'Grady had come clean. It was almost as if she'd walked into the meeting intending to confess.

He changed the subject again. "Did you get the

message that Stevie wants to talk to both of us tonight?" he said.

"Yeah, I did. Is there a time that's good for you? He says he can merge the call so we can all talk at the same time."

Jeff looked at the top of his phone. It was just after six. Dinner would be ready soon and he had some homework he had to get done. "How's eight o'clock?" he said.

"Perfect," she answered. "We can both finish our homework."

As usual, she was a step ahead of him.

Jeff's phone rang at 8:01. Stevie already had Andi on the line. "Andi says you have something you need to tell me that happened today," he said. "First, let me update you guys on what I've done."

He said he'd found six middle school girls whose coaches were certain had been contacted by agents. At least three, he said, had either expressed interest or had made deals of some kind—written or unwritten— with agents. He'd give them details when he saw them next.

The best—or most important—he saved for last. Terri Porter had returned his call the previous night.

He'd been totally straight with her and told her he'd talked to Andi about agents pursuing her.

"The first thing she said when I told her that was, 'No kidding. Did you know the sun's going to rise in the east tomorrow morning?' But then she said she'd talk to her brother and try to arrange for the three of us to meet this coming weekend. They have matches tomorrow and Friday—just like you guys do. I suggested Andy's on Saturday. I know you guys both like the place."

"You think that's safe?" Jeff asked. "You don't think we might be followed?"

"What if we are?" Andi said. "We don't have anything to hide and neither do they."

"Except maybe from their crazy father," Jeff said.

"Well, neither one of them had ever heard of Andy's," Steve said. "So, I suspect their father hasn't either."

"How will they get there?" Jeff asked.

"Uber," Steve said. "I told them I'd gladly reimburse them if need be."

"Where does this leave us, then?" Andi asked.

Steve didn't answer for a moment. Then, quietly he said, "On the trail of a damn good story, I suspect. If it makes you feel better, Andi, I think this one goes way beyond you."

"Good," Andi said. "Very good."

It was then Jeff's turn to tell Stevie what had happened earlier that day.

Somehow, the word that Joan O'Grady was no longer coaching the tennis team had become common knowledge at school by lunchtime the next day. To Andi, it felt like everywhere she turned, someone was making a crack about the coach's sudden departure.

"What is it with you and coaches, Carillo?" was a common theme.

Andi was beginning to wonder that a little bit herself. She'd been involved in a very public battle with her soccer coach; had led a coup d'état to overthrow her basketball coach, and now, midway through the season, her tennis coach had quit—and, without even knowing it, she had played a major role in her departure—or ouster, depending on your point of view. The only difference, she reasoned, was that she had never exchanged a single angry word with Coach O'Grady. She liked her—a lot—which made this hurt more. Knowing that Coach O'Grady's encouragement and kindness was part of a scheme to woo her for Aces Inc. made her sad.

Jeff, Maria Medley, and Eleanor Dove were all waiting for her at their usual table during the lunch period.

"So, O'Grady was really an agent disguised in teacher's clothing," Maria said before Andi had a chance to even put a napkin in her lap. "Another season, another really bad coach."

It figured, Andi thought, that Maria already knew the whole story. No one had more friends at Merion Middle than Maria. She was outgoing—to the max—and the kind of person people *wanted* to tell secrets to.

Eleanor, Maria's best friend, was a foot taller and quieter, but equally smart. "You really are three-for-three, aren't you?" she said as Andi tried to act as if the pasta she was trying to eat was the greatest meal she'd ever had. "First you get a misogynist soccer coach who doesn't want girls playing with boys. Then you get a racist basketball coach who doesn't know how to coach basketball. And now you get a tennis coach who sees you as some kind of human ATM machine. You really do have a knack."

She was smiling when she said it and was clearly being sympathetic. But being reminded of it all made Andi feel a little bit sick. She put her fork down, took a long sip of water, and shook her head.

"Am I really that bad a person?" she asked.

All three of them laughed and Jeff said, "No, Andi, you really are that good an athlete. You're the Natural without the baseball bat."

Andi remembered the Robert Redford movie in

which the actor played an aging baseball player making a comeback after being shot and finds himself surrounded by all sorts of corruption.

"Well," she said, "I guess the good news is no one's tried to shoot me."

"Yet," Maria said. She was—clearly—joking.

Andi was having trouble finding anything funny at that moment.

23

THERE WAS ONLY ONE COACH—COACH FOSTER—ON THE TEAM bus heading to Main Line that afternoon. Before the bus left, Coach Foster told the team he hoped to have a new co-coach in time for Friday's match against Haverford. He also announced the lineup for that day. There was only one change: Jeff Michaels and Gary Morrissey switching off at number one and number two boys' singles. No one reacted to that as the bus pulled away.

Except for Gary, who walked back two rows and sat down in the empty seat next to Jeff. "So . . . I talked to my dad last night," he said. "I want you to know I didn't know anything about what was going on."

"I figured," Jeff said. "I could tell yesterday when we were warming up. It never occurred to me that you knew anything."

For a moment, Gary said nothing. Then he said, "Why do you think she confessed? All she had to do was move you back to number one and that would have been it. No one would have known what she was really up to."

Jeff and Andi had talked about that already. "What did your dad say about it last night?" he asked. "Did he have any ideas?"

Gary shook his head. "All he said was the company wasn't going to recruit Andi anymore."

"You believe him?" Jeff said.

Gary said nothing. Finally, he stood up and said, "Put it this way. I *want* to believe him."

They arrived a couple minutes later. The trip down Route 1 to Main Line wasn't a long one and the rush hour traffic hadn't really gotten bad yet. It was a spectacular spring day and Jeff was so fired up to play, he felt as if he could hold his own with Federer or Djokovic or Nadal. Well, maybe not Nadal on clay.

Still, as they walked to the courts, he could tell by Andi's body language that she didn't feel the same way. "You okay?" he asked.

"I'm fine, I guess," she said. "I'm just a little worn out by all the drama in my life. I just want to *play*, not spend my life trying to figure out which bad guy is up to what."

Jeff understood. "Well, for the rest of the afternoon, all you have to do is play," he said.

She unzipped her racquet cover and gave him her best smile. "You know what, you're right," she said. "Let's just play and whip these guys."

She and Jeff exchanged a high five and headed for the courts.

Whether it was Jeff's little pep talk, the beautiful spring day, or just telling herself to focus strictly on tennis, Andi played as well as she had played in at least a couple of weeks. Her poor opponent, Rachel Feinman, had no chance. She had managed to win three games against Andi the first time they played; this time she won one.

Andi's first serve seemed to go in every time and, because she felt so confident, she consistently followed it to net. When Feinman was able to get a return back, Andi was there to pounce on a volley and end the point quickly. It wasn't all that different when Feinman served. Andi kept her pinned in the backcourt even when she got a first serve in and jumped all over her second serve to quickly end those points. The match took forty-five minutes. Andi was a little annoyed when, leading 5–0 in the second set, she missed a couple of easy forehands and allowed Feinman to win a game.

As they shook hands, Feinman said, "It was nice

of you to give me that game so you wouldn't double bagel me."

Double bageled meant winning a match without losing a game.

Andi gave Feinman a semi-fierce look. "I didn't give you the game," she said. "You earned it."

She remembered playing a match when she was nine and still learning how to compete. She'd lost by the same score that she'd just won by, 6–0, 6–1. When they shook hands at the net, the girl who'd beaten her said, "Nice of me to let you win a game."

Andi had wanted to punch her. She couldn't even acknowledge that Andi had taken a game off her. She *knew* the girl had been trying for the double bagel. She'd been doing the same thing and didn't want Feinman to think she hadn't deserved to win the game she won.

As they came off court, Andi glanced at the next court and saw that Jeff was down a set and was tied 3–all in the second. The last thing Jeff needed was to lose right after being restored to the number one slot. She could see that Gary was up a set and a break in his match. So was Lisa Carmichael, playing girls number two. The number three matches were being played on the other side of a fence so she couldn't see the scores there, but she noticed Coach Foster and the doubles players watching Jeff's match. That would indicate this was the most difficult predicament any of the Merion players were facing.

She walked over to join her teammates standing behind the court. As she walked up, Mindy Garceau whispered, "break point," nodding at Jeff, who was serving from the far court. Jeff twisted in what Andi assumed was a second serve and then, much to Andi's surprise, charged the net. Jeff didn't come in often, especially behind a second serve. But the move caught his opponent off guard. He took his eye off the ball for an instant and his return wobbled off the side of his racquet. Jeff had an easy volley and put it away as his teammates cheered lustily.

"Bullet dodged," Mindy whispered.

"Gutsy play," Andi answered.

Jeff held from there. His opponent, whose name, according to Coach Foster, was Trey Spanarkel, was clearly upset with himself for blowing the break point. Then, serving at 3–4, he double-faulted twice to give Jeff three break points. Spanarkel saved the first two with service winners, but at 30–40, Jeff got a good deep return and then fooled Spanarkel with a drop shot. The Main Line number one charged in and barely got his racquet on the ball, pushing it into the net. He stood and waved his racquet in Jeff's direction, saluting the good shot.

Jeff served the set out from there.

The third set was back-and-forth. Jeff broke serve in the opening game and it looked like he'd gained control of the match. Then Spanarkel broke right back, held, and broke Jeff again to lead 3–1. Jeff then won the next two games to make it 3–all.

"Feels like the next guy to *hold* serve twice in a row is going to win," Mindy said to Andi, who was so tense at that moment she couldn't come up with any sort of response.

As it turned out, Mindy was right. Both players held to 4–all and then Jeff became the first player to hold twice in a row in the set—serving two aces at deuce—both up the middle with Spanarkel leaning into the alley. Serving at 4–5, Spanarkel's nerves kicked in again. Up 30–15, he served a double fault, going for too much with Jeff creeping in on his second serve. Then he netted an easy backhand, allowing Jeff to get to match point. He went for a big first serve and missed. Jeff crept in again, ran around a serve aimed wide so he could hit a forehand, and crushed the ball perfectly into the corner. Spanarkel took one step to go after it, stopped, pivoted, and jogged to net to shake Jeff's hand.

Jeff's teammates spilled onto the court to congratulate him as if he had scored the clinching point. In fact, his win gave the Mustangs a clean sweep in the singles. Soon after, both the boys and the girls won their doubles matches in straight sets and Merion had an 8–0 win to raise its season record to 6–1.

"Easy sweep for the good guys, huh?" Andi said to Jeff, who was smiling for what felt like the first time in a month.

"Speak for yourself," Jeff said. "The only thing easy about my match was the handshake. Spanarkel's a nice guy."

They both laughed. It had also been a while, Andi thought, since they'd done that.

24

"THE STORY IS THERE, NO DOUBT IT'S THERE. THE QUESTION is what form should it take and how deep can we go with it?"

Stevie Thomas and Jeff were already well into their first slices of pizza. Andi was waiting for hers to cool a little, grinning at the remarkable appetites of teenage and preteen boys.

After ordering their pizzas, they had spent the waiting time reviewing Friday's match against Haverford. It had been easier than expected, given that the earlier match had almost required a mixed doubles match before Merion had won 5–3. In fact, Jeff had almost been hoping for a 4–4 split so he would finally get to play mixed with Andi.

But Andi and Lisa Carmichael, who had become an

unbeatable combination playing 1–2 on the girls' side, had won their matches easily while Jeff and Gary had won their matches—not easily. Both had needed three sets but had come away with victories. When Jane Blythe had also won a three-setter at the girls' number three, Merion had an insurmountable 5–0 lead. Tommy Arnold had lost the boys' number three match and the doubles matches had been split, giving Merion a 6–2 victory.

Villanova had also won and remained unbeaten.

"Let's say you and Villanova win out and you guys win the rematch," Stevie had asked. "How do they break the tie?"

Andi grinned. "Mixed doubles," she said.

Stevie smiled. "So, it would be you and Jeff playing together with the whole season on the line?"

"I *hope* it would be the two of us playing together with the whole season on the line," Jeff said.

"It better be," Andi said. "Or Coach Foster and Coach Wentworth might not live to see the match."

On Thursday, Janelle Wentworth had been named Coach Foster's assistant coach for the remainder of the season. She was a PE teacher who, like O'Grady, had played college tennis. Unlike O'Grady she wasn't trying to stealth-recruit Andi to sign with an agent.

"At least as far as we know," Jeff said when they

had finished filling Stevie in on the little they knew about their new coach.

"Why assistant coach?" Stevie asked. "Why not co-coach like with O'Grady?"

"How'd that work out?" Andi asked. Then, more seriously, she said, "Coach Foster's been with us all season. Coach Wentworth is learning on the fly with only four matches left in the season. It makes sense."

Once they had picked up their pizzas, the subject quickly changed to where to go next with the story on agents recruiting preteens. Stevie had gotten the Porters to agree to meet him for lunch the next day. He had told them he was working on a story about tennis prodigies.

"Which has the great benefit of being the truth," he said. "Andi being there will fit in since she's a prodigy, too."

"So, does that mean I can't come?" Jeff said. "I'm clearly not a prodigy."

"You're my assistant, my intern," Stevie said. "I'm letting you help out on some stories as a favor to your dad."

"And Tyler and Terri are getting away from their dad how?" Andi asked.

Stevie grinned. "Their father's out of town, some kind of business trip," he said. "They'll tell their mother they're going to practice and walk down to the public courts near their house. I'll pick them up there."

"Any chance Mom will come down to watch at some point?" Andi asked.

Stevie smiled. "You will make a good reporter someday, Andi," he said.

"Hey," Jeff said, "I'm your intern. I was about to ask that."

"Mom feels as if tennis is going to take her children away from her when they go to IMG Academy in the fall. She has no interest in watching them play."

"So where are we meeting for lunch?" Jeff asked.

Stevie shrugged. "Where else? At your office."

"You mean here? Works for me."

"We could get cheesesteaks again," Andi said. She really liked a good cheesesteak.

"I already told them pizza," Stevie said. "They seemed happy with that idea."

So was Jeff.

Andi sighed. "Maybe next time," she said.

Jeff filled his dad in late that afternoon on the Porter plan. They were on their way to the Wells Fargo Center for a Flyers' playoff game against the Islanders. Normally, it would be impossible for Jeff to go with his dad to a game this important. But his father had convinced his bosses that he could use someone to take notes for him in the Islanders' postgame locker room while he and his camera crew were in the Flyers' locker room.

So, Jeff had a media credential dangling from his neck as they walked into the building and headed for the elevator that would take them to the sky-high press box that almost literally scraped the building's ceiling.

His dad paid $26 for two pre-game meals, getting a receipt for one so he could expense it.

"There was a time," he said, "when the media ate free most places. Not so much anymore."

"Is that wrong?" Jeff asked.

"Actually, it's not," his dad said. "If I wasn't working tonight, no one would be giving me a free meal someplace. The old theory was that teams *needed* media coverage, so they paid for those who covered them to eat. Now, no one thinks that way."

Jeff looked at the chicken breasts on his plate. "Is this worth thirteen bucks?" he asked.

His dad laughed. "Absolutely not," he said. "But trust me, the food at the concession stands is a lot more overpriced than this."

They picked up drinks and found a place to sit.

"Two internships in one day," Jeff said as they sat down. "First with Stevie for the *Daily News* and now with you. Pretty good I think."

"Don't get cocky," his dad said. "So far, as an intern, you've accomplished exactly nothing except costing me thirteen dollars for that food."

Jeff took a long sip of Coke. "So, what do you want me to do?"

"Tonight's easy," his dad said. "You go to the Islanders' locker room and, depending on how the game goes, get me a quote or two I can use as part of my postgame stand-up. Take your phone and record everything so the quotes will be accurate. If a guy scores a game-winning goal, you'll probably get a quote saying all the credit should go to his teammates."

Jeff figured he could handle that.

"What you're going to do with Stevie tomorrow is far more important," his dad continued. "But you'll have Stevie there, so I suspect you'll be fine."

The Islanders won 3–2 on an overtime goal by Anders Lee. Jeff got to his locker just as he started to talk about the game-winning goal. "The guys set me up," he said. "They deserve all the credit."

25

THE PORTER TWINS WERE ALREADY SITTING AT A TABLE AT 10:55 the next morning when Andi and Jeff arrived. Stevie was nowhere in sight.

The twins stood up and, as if to make sure they weren't worried, Terri said, "Stevie's here. He just went to the men's room. Can't order pizza until eleven o'clock."

Andi was struck again by how tall *and* attractive they both were. Tyler was at least six foot two and his twin sister was five-eleven if she was an inch. They both had dimples when they smiled and bright brown eyes. She could tell by the way Jeff was staring at Terri that he was thinking the same thing.

Stevie arrived, apologizing for the delay.

"I think we can order," he said, pointing out a woman standing at the cash register. "Let's get going before there's a line."

Pizzas ordered, sodas opened, they all sat down.

"I know you all know each other," Stevie said. "And I know three of you have been dealing with the pressures that come with being very good at a sport at a very young age. So, I thought it would be good to talk to you."

"Mr. Thomas . . ." Tyler began.

"Steve," he said. "Or Stevie, whichever you prefer. My byline is Steve, but my friends call me Stevie."

"Okay then, Stevie," Tyler said. "We're a little nervous about this. Our dad probably wouldn't be very happy if we talked to you about some of the things we've experienced."

"And some of the things we've experienced because of him," Terri added. "Especially those things."

Stevie was nodding his head. "I get it, totally get it," he said. "Why don't we say that, for now, everything you tell me is off the record. I need information more than I need quotes."

"What exactly is off the record?" Tyler asked.

Jeff often forgot that most people had no idea what journalism terms meant.

"It means he's only looking for names and stories he can check out," Andi said. "He won't use your names unless you give him permission to later on."

"Is that right?" Terri said, looking at Stevie.

"Exactly right," Stevie said.

She looked directly at Andi. "Do you trust him?" she asked bluntly.

"Completely," Andi said. "He worked on stories I was involved in during soccer and basketball seasons and was always as good as his word."

Tyler looked at Jeff. "No offense, but why is he here? I mean, is he getting attention from agents, too?"

Jeff laughed. "Only because I'm Andi's friend," he said.

Stevie nodded again. "You're right, Tyler, he's not in your class or Andi's but he has been approached because he's Andi's friend. He's also the son of a prominent TV reporter in town so he knows how to be a reporter, and I've asked him to help me out."

"Your father is Tom Michaels, right?" Terri said. "The guy who covers the Eagles for Comcast?"

"NBC Sports–Philly," Jeff said, unable to resist the correction. The name had been changed several years earlier but most people still thought of the station as Comcast SportsNet. "But yes, that's my dad. And he does cover the Eagles a lot."

There was a moment of silence at the table. They heard their names being called. The pizza was ready. The question, Andi thought, was whether the Porters were ready.

* * *

As it turned out, once they understood that they weren't going to be quoted, the Porters were very willing to talk. And, they had a lot to say.

Often, one would start a story and the other would finish it. Or the person not telling the story would fill in details.

"It started when we turned ten," Terri said. "I was ranked number three nationally in the ten-and-unders and Tyler was—"

"Eleventh," Tyler said. "Back then she was still taller than me—"

"And stronger. He was really skinny. At first, the agents and equipment reps were only interested in me. It wasn't until a couple years later when Tyler started to grow, they started getting interested in him."

"Even so, it's always been more about her," Tyler said. "The interest in me was more about being her twin."

Jeff had actually put down his pizza when Terri said the agents had first approached when she was ten.

"Ten?" he said. "Seriously? Ten?"

"Maybe a little unusual," Terri said. "But hardly unique. Our dad showed us an old TV show from the PBS station here in Philadelphia. It was when Venus was ten and Serena was nine. They were on-camera with their dad and they're all wearing Reebok.

"There was a reporter on the show and he asked Mr. Williams where they'd gotten all the Reebok gear.

He just smiled and said, 'Oh, Reebok is a very nice company.'"

"Serena was nine?" Stevie asked, apparently wanting to be sure.

"Yup," Terri said.

"So, who approached you?" Andi asked.

"No one approached us," Terri said. "They approached my dad. I guess these people do their homework. They figured dad would be willing to listen."

"Was he?" Stevie asked.

They both laughed. "Are you kidding?" Tyler said. "By the time we were eleven, we were practically calling Lee Crenshaw and Sarah Waxman Uncle Lee and Aunt Sarah."

"They're our agents," Terri added. "We both have deals with clothing companies, racquet companies, and a couple of tennis clubs."

"Half the money we've been paid is in a trust fund our dad started," Tyler added.

"And the other half?" Stevie asked.

"Why don't you check and see how much my dad has worked as a recreation director the last three years," Terri said.

"Does he have a job at all?" Andi asked.

"Absolutely," Terri said, unable to suppress a laugh. "He is a junior talent scout for Aces Inc. He's brought them two juniors with tremendous potential."

Stevie sat back in his chair. "The old Earl Woods trick," he said.

"What does that mean?" Andi and Jeff asked at the same moment.

"When Tiger Woods was a teenager and still an amateur who couldn't legally have an agent, his father was on IMG's payroll as a junior talent scout," Stevie said. "The day Tiger turned pro, you'll never guess who he signed with as his representatives."

"Speaking of that, you guys are still playing amateur tennis," Andi said. "How can you be getting paid?"

"We aren't getting paid," Tyler said. "Everyone pays Aces, and they pay my dad—their junior talent scout. We haven't been paid a cent."

"Technically speaking," Andi said.

"Exactly," Terri answered.

"But what about having an agent?" Terri said.

Tyler leaned forward and gave her a bright smile. "Who said we have an agent? Our dad just happens to work for an agent."

They were all silent for a moment, Stevie, Andi, and Jeff each trying to wrap their minds around what they'd just been told.

"Where does IMG Academy fit in to all this?" Stevie finally asked.

"Aces Inc. gets paid a finder's fee for delivering two budding stars," Tyler said. "We pay no tuition and, whenever we turn pro, we already have a contract in place saying we'll be repped by Aces. Doesn't mean at some point IMG won't come after us if we become real stars and moneymakers, but Aces has first crack."

"They've had first crack since we were ten," Terri added.

"Anyone else come after you back then?" Andi asked, remembering her recent experiences with ProStyles and New Advantage.

"Oh yeah," Terri said. "Difference was, Aces Inc. was willing to pay my dad money up front. They were just starting out. The others were more standard: you make big money when we make big money. Dad took the money up front."

"Does Aces have this sort of deal with anyone else?" Stevie asked, an instant before Jeff did.

"I'm sure they do," Tyler said. "But we don't know names."

The pizza was gone. It was time to get to work.

26

IT WAS ALMOST HARD TO BELIEVE THERE WERE ONLY FOUR matches left in the tennis season. To Jeff and Andi it felt as if tryouts for the team had been about fifteen minutes ago.

"That's because we've been so preoccupied with everything else, time's flown by," Andi said Monday at lunch. "We've got four matches to play in ten days. But we also have a lot of work to do."

They had agreed not to talk about the progress of the story in front of others and so, when Danny Diskin, Eleanor Dove, and Maria Medley joined them, they changed the subject to the next day's match with King of Prussia. Villanova had beaten KOP 5–4 on Friday, which meant two things: Merion needed to keep winning if it wanted the final match of the season against

Villanova to mean anything, and KOP was going to be a tough out.

"They were tough the first time around, weren't they?" Danny asked after Andi had laid out the current situation for everyone.

"We had to go to the mixed doubles tiebreaker to win," Andi said. "Fortunately, they made a mistake and went with two doubles players who weren't all that good, and Gary and I won pretty easily. If we get to mixed, I doubt they'll make the same mistake again."

"And you won't be playing with Gary again if there's a mixed doubles match," Jeff said. He wanted to be sure everyone understood that. Actually, as long as the coaches understood it, he was fine.

They bussed through traffic to get to KOP, which was across the street from the massive King of Prussia mall and on the same campus as the high school. There were eight tennis courts right next to the football stadium, which looked to be big enough to house a small college football team.

As he warmed up with Gary, Jeff remembered how badly Gary had been beaten in the first match by Dickie Weiss, KOP's number one. He suspected he would be in for a tough afternoon. KOP's number two, James Mayer, had taken Jeff to three sets and Jeff knew he would be a tough out for Gary. It occurred to him that it might be up to the girls to carry the boys today.

He wasn't wrong. Dickie Weiss wasn't ranked fifth in the East without good reason. Jeff actually played well, taking the first set to a tiebreak and even had a set point at 6–5. But Weiss blew two serves past him and then smashed a backhand return that Jeff couldn't touch to win the tiebreak, 8–6, and the set, 7–6. Emotionally, Jeff had needed to win the set because he knew the chances he'd come that close in one set, lose it, and *then* win two more were slim. He hung in for a while in the second set before Weiss simply stopped missing anything—or so it seemed to Jeff. The KOP number one broke him at 3–all, held easily, and then broke again to win the set 6–3. Jeff's consolation was he had played very competitively with a very good player. The result, however, wasn't going to help his team win.

The result of the number two singles match wasn't going to help, either. Jeff knew that James Mayer was a good player, he'd beaten him in three tough sets, but he was surprised at how easily he beat Gary Morrissey. The match wasn't as close as Jeff's match with Weiss, Mayer winning, 6–3, 6–3.

"I swear he didn't miss a first serve," Gary said when Jeff came off the court after his match. Jeff remembered Mayer's serve and knew Gary wasn't wrong about how tough it was to handle. Still, he'd have thought the match would be closer. There was no point in commenting though so he just asked, "How are the rest of the matches going?"

Gary reported that Andi and Lisa Carmichael had both won and the number three singles matches were both in the third set. The doubles were just starting.

"I'm betting you get to make your debut in mixed doubles today," Gary said. He almost sounded relieved.

They walked over to join Andi, who was watching Jane Blythe's match. Jane had just broken serve to go up 4–2 in the third. Unfortunately, Art Schnabel, playing next to Jane's court, had just lost his serve to go down 3–2.

"You ready to play again?" he asked.

"Actually, dying to play again," she answered. "Especially with you as my partner."

Jeff wasn't sure if that was a tennis comment or a personal comment. He didn't really care.

Blythe went on to win and Schnabel, after breaking back to 5–all, lost in a tiebreak. Merion won the girls' doubles match; lost the boys. That meant it was 4–4—the girls having won all their matches; the boys having lost all of theirs. Jeff remembered that KOP had made the mistake the last time they played of sending two doubles players out for the deciding mixed doubles and Andi and Gary had crushed them, 8–1. He was certain they wouldn't make the same mistake twice.

Sure enough, when he and Andi walked back on court after a brief pep talk from Coach Foster, Dickie Weiss was waiting along with Molly Adler, KOP's number one singles player, who Andi had twice beaten easily. It appeared KOP had the stronger boy, Merion the stronger girl. But mixed doubles was a lot different than singles; different skills came into play. Weiss, Jeff had noticed, was strictly a backcourt player. He was not. He hoped his ability at the net would make up for Weiss's strong ground game.

All four players held their serve the first time around. But at 2–all, with Weiss serving, Adler twice dumped easy volleys into the net, giving Jeff and Andi a break point.

"Hit your return right at her," Andi hissed as Jeff walked back to receive serve. Weiss's first serve was long. Jeff guessed he'd try to spin the second serve to his backhand and jumped into the doubles alley as soon as he tossed the ball so he could hit a forehand return. He wound up and hit it as hard as he could, directly at Adler. He heard her scream as she tried to fend the ball off as it came right at her. The ball hit her racquet frame and bounced into the net.

Andi raced over for a high five. With a big smile on

his face, Jeff walked to the side of the court to change ends. Weiss hadn't even bothered to grab a towel. He came straight at Jeff, pointing his racquet at him.

"You try to hit my partner like that again and I'll deck you right here!" he said in a voice that could probably be heard all the way up and down Route 1.

"I wasn't trying to hit her," Jeff said. "I was trying to win the point. I was in the backcourt, for crying out loud. Not my fault you hit a puffball second serve."

The last sentence was a mistake. Weiss threw his racquet down and advanced on Jeff. He was a couple inches taller and probably a good twenty pounds heavier. Andi quickly jumped in between the two boys.

"Are you nuts?" she said to Weiss. "We're playing tennis here, not football."

The coaches came running in quickly. Weiss was still glaring at Jeff but clearly wasn't going to try to go through Andi to get to him.

"Hey, everyone, let's calm down," Jeff heard Coach Foster say.

"Like Miss Carillo said, we're playing tennis here," said KOP's coach, a woman who Jeff guessed was about thirty.

She turned to Coach Foster. "I do think an apology is called for. It certainly looked like your player was trying to hit my player."

Coach Foster looked at her as if she had grown a second head. "On a service return?" he said. "Novak Djokovic isn't *that* good. We're talking about an eleven-year-old kid here, who came up with a terrific return that happened to go right at your player. No one was hurt. *Your* guy should apologize for making a big deal out of it because he was embarrassed about losing his serve."

Before things could get any more heated, KOP's other coach came running up and threw an arm around his colleague. "Jennifer, let's just let the kids play, okay?" he said. "Everyone agree?"

No one argued.

Jeff turned to go pick up a couple of balls, so he could serve. "Three–two," he said in a loud voice. "Let me know when you're ready."

He had his back to the two KOP players as he walked to the baseline, but he could almost feel Weiss trying to glare a hole through him. He picked the balls up from the back wall and turned to get into position to serve. Andi had taken her position at the net. Slowly, Weiss and Adler got into position. He waited for Adler to signal that she was ready. When she didn't put her hand up to indicate she was ready to play, he said, "Just let me know when you're ready."

She waited a moment, then put her hand up to tell

Jeff she was ready. Jeff slammed a perfect ace down the middle. He'd never felt better about a serve.

He held at love. They then broke Adler to lead 5–2. Weiss appeared to have given up. Andi held easily and Weiss, clearly just wanting to get the match over with, served three double faults. He got one serve in—a push that landed in the middle of the service box, leaving Andi with an easy forehand, which she aimed right at Adler's feet.

As the ball skipped past Adler to end the game, she looked at Weiss and said, "That okay with you, Dickie? Was I delicate enough?"

Weiss said nothing. They changed sides one last time and Jeff served out the match, Merion winning the set, 8–2. Adler came to net to shake hands. Weiss did not. The two KOP coaches were standing next to the players' chairs. "Go back and shake hands," the female coach said.

Weiss looked at her coaching companion. He just pointed in the direction of the net where the other three players were standing. Slowly, Weiss walked back to offer a less-than-hearty handshake to the two winners.

"Nice playing, you guys," Adler said rather pointedly. Then she walked away, casting a disgusted look at Weiss.

The rest of the Merion team raced on court to congratulate Jeff and Andi.

"How much fun was that?" Jeff said to Andi.

"Never enjoyed a win more," Andi said.

Jeff knew she'd had some very good wins in the past. He also knew she was 100 percent sincere.

27

STEVIE THOMAS WAS TALKING TO JEFF OUTSIDE THE GIRLS' locker room when Andi, who had treated herself to a long shower, walked through the door.

"What'd you do in there, stop and finish your homework?" Jeff asked.

Andi laughed. "Didn't know anyone was waiting for me. What's up, Stevie?"

"Let's go sit for a minute," Stevie said. "I assume your rides will be here soon."

They went and sat on the bench next to the circle so they could spot their parents—Andi's dad, Jeff's mom—when they pulled up. Jeff had already texted his mom asking for a few extra minutes when he saw Stevie. Andi had told her dad she would be a while, too, because of her lengthy shower. Her hair was tied into a wet ponytail. Jeff thought she looked spectacular.

"I talked to your dad this afternoon," Stevie said, nodding at Jeff. "You know he's at Villanova–Temple tonight, right?"

Jeff knew. He'd wanted to go but it was a nine o'clock game—for TV of course—on a school night.

"He's talked to a bunch of agents who willingly admit that recruiting kids as young as Andi is part of the job, although none of them are actually the recruiters. He also talked directly to Tad Walters, who wasn't willing to go on camera and Renee Stubing—who was."

"Figures," Andi said. "She thinks she can charm her way past anyone."

"And she probably can," Stevie said. "She's not going to admit that kids or their dads are paid the way the Porter twins are paid—certainly not by her company. She might be willing, at least off camera, to point fingers at some others."

"But then they'll just deny it," Jeff said.

Stevie nodded. "Of course they will." He paused. "You guys know who Bobby Kelleher is?"

They didn't.

"He's been my mentor since I started trying to be a reporter," Stevie said. "His mentor was Bob Woodward. You *have* heard of him, right?"

They both nodded. Woodward was arguably the most famous reporter ever, half of the *Washington Post* reporting team that had written the stories that led to

Richard Nixon becoming the only man to resign the presidency.

"Woodward always told Bobby—and Bobby always tells me—'Get the documents and you get the story.'"

Seeing the puzzled looks on Andi's and Jeff's faces, he plowed on. "Somewhere, there's written evidence of Aces Inc. paying the Porter kids—whether through the father or not. And, if we can get Stubing or anyone else to point fingers at other agents doing this, there will be documents somewhere proving what they're doing. We get the documents, we've got the story."

"How do we do that?" Jeff said. "It's not like we can just ask for them."

"No, we can't," Stevie said. "But then again, yes we can."

He looked at Andi. "*If* you're up for doing some undercover work."

Stevie Thomas and Tom Michaels had already talked their plan through that afternoon. But they still needed to discuss it with Andi and her parents. All three would need to be involved.

The earliest it would be possible to get everyone together was Saturday. Andi and Jeff were dying to get moving sooner, but there was no way to do that. They had school—and a match with Bryn Mawr on

Friday. Stevie had two finals to take. And Andi's and Jeff's parents all had jobs.

So, it was decided the meeting would take place Saturday. Jeff and Andi got to choose the location. In a major upset, Andi suggested a mom-and-pop ice cream place near her favorite tennis equipment store, where she was having a racquet restrung. "My dad really likes the milkshakes," she said. Jeff didn't argue. He loved milkshakes—and he needed to pick up some grip tape, too.

They took over a large table in a corner of the restaurant where they could all sit. Once everyone had arrived and ordered, the two reporters took turns updating the others. When Stevie finished his update on the Porters, who Andi and Jeff would be facing in the final match of the season the following Friday, Andi said: "So, what's your plan?"

Before he could answer, Tom Michaels looked at Andi's mom and dad. "For the record, speaking as a parent, I completely understand if you don't want Andi to do this."

Stevie nodded and added, "For the record, speaking as a non-parent, I understand what Tom is saying."

"And?" Andi said. She was feeling a little impatient. So far, the meeting had just been a recycling of what they already knew, and now Jeff's dad and Stevie were telling her and her parents why they shouldn't go forward with the plan they were about to propose.

Stevie put up a hand. "Got it," he said. "Here's the deal. We need to get documentation to back up what Tyler and Terri have told us about their father's deal with Aces Inc. Clearly, neither Aces nor Papa Porter are going to hand over their contracts."

More telling us what we already know, Andi thought. Stevie read her body language.

"I'm getting to it, Andi," he said, and smiled. "Patience not your strength, is it?" Without waiting for her to answer, he plowed on. "Andi, you need to get in touch with your former coach, Ms. O'Grady. Find her at school on Monday and tell her that you've talked to the Porters and they blew you away with the kind of money they claimed to be making. Be sure to say, 'claimed.' You need to sound as if you're still skeptical. You might even say you haven't talked to your parents about it yet, because you want to know if it's true before you guys get serious about talking to them."

"Do you really think she'll bite?" Andi's dad said.

Stevie looked at Jeff's dad. "I've never met an agent who wasn't willing to do almost anything to get a client who they thought might be worth big bucks," he said. "That includes the ones I'd call 'good guys.' Good being a relative term."

"But she's not really an agent," Jeff said.

"Not *yet*," Stevie answered. "She *wants* to be an agent, which probably makes her even more eager. Bringing you in was the carrot they put in front of her, right? This might be her chance to get back in the ball game."

"Or to get the job she badly wants," Tom Michaels added.

Andi looked at her parents. For once, she wanted to know how they felt before she made a decision.

"What's the downside in this?" her mother said.

Stevie looked at Mr. Michaels.

"History says agents don't take it well if they feel they've been burned in some way. Usually, it has to do with money. Someone leaves them for another agent, or a deal goes away for some reason. This is different, but if we embarrass them publicly by revealing what they're doing, they definitely won't take it well."

"Chances are, though, they'll attack the media—as in Tom and me," Stevie added.

"But they could go after the athlete—in this case Andi, right?" her dad said. "Wasn't there that deal a while back with Zion Williamson when he changed agents?"

The reference, as Jeff remembered it, was to the superstar basketball player who had dumped one agency for another almost as soon as he'd become the number one pick in the NBA draft after playing at Duke for one year.

"Yeah, that did happen," Mr. Michaels said. "When he left, the spurned agents filed a lawsuit, making all sorts of wild accusations against Williamson, against Duke, and against various sponsors who were paying the kid. It never went anywhere; it was just flailing."

"But to be fair," Stevie added, "the story got a lot more play in the media than it deserved." He paused, about to admit something—as a non-Duke fan—he didn't want to admit: "A lot of it was just because so many people are jealous of Duke and Mike Krzyzewski. They *wanted* the story to be true. I doubt anything like that will happen with Andi."

"Stevie's right," Tom Michaels said. "They won't come after us. Attacking an eleven-year-old girl won't look good—no matter what."

There was silence for a moment. Andi realized everyone was looking at her. She shrugged. "I'm game," she said, then smiled. "In fact, I kind of like the idea."

Stevie and Tom Michaels both nodded. "We have to get the Aces people to produce a contract like the Porters' for Andi and her parents to sign," Stevie said. "If we can get that, I'll bet the Porters will go on the record."

"Then we get the Stubing woman to go on camera and brag about how she *doesn't* recruit tennis players,"

Tom Michaels said. "And I'll bet we can find plenty of people in tennis who will say this goes on. Difference is, we'll have specifics, not just generalities."

"And," Andi said with a smile, "we'll have the documents."

"Bob Woodward will be proud," Stevie said.

Their order arrived. Jeff was ready for his milkshake. Andi was ready to take the next step.

28

ANDI WAS TEMPTED TO EMAIL JOAN O'GRADY TO SET UP A
time to meet her, but Jeff discouraged that idea. "She
might ignore it or say no," he said. "Just show up."

Andi decided he was right. Knowing that most
teachers were in their classrooms prior to the start of
first period at 8:30, she found her way to room 227 by
8:15 on Monday morning. The door was open, and Ms.
O'Grady was sitting at her desk reading what looked
like test papers. When she saw Andi in the doorway,
she almost did a double take.

"Are you lost, Ms. Carillo?" she said, a genuine
question mark in her voice.

Andi smiled. "No, I'm not," she said. "May I come in
for a minute?"

Ms. O'Grady glanced at her watch, then put down

her pen and waved her into the room. "Please," she said. "What can I do for you?"

Andi wanted to be polite, but not to come across as timid. She had made a major decision and now she was seeking guidance on what to do next.

She took a chair from the front row and pushed it forward so it was next to Ms. O'Grady's desk. Ms. O'Grady folded her arms, smiled, and said, "The floor is yours."

Andi waited a beat—intentionally—took a deep breath, and then began talking very fast—which was also intentional.

"I spent some time with the Porter twins this past weekend," she said, causing Ms. O'Grady's eyebrows to go up and her eyes to widen. Not wanting to pause long enough for a question, Andi kept going. "I know they're planning to go to IMG in the fall, and it was pretty apparent that their dad is very involved in everything they do. I was curious about how they landed at IMG and what was involved."

"Did they tell you?" Ms. O'Grady said, a little bit of fear creeping into her voice.

"Yes," Andi said, as if she'd been asked if she liked playing tennis. "Honestly, I had no idea. I mean, I heard the various agents talking about making money, but I really didn't understand at all. And the way they're doing it is, well, so smart. If they keep getting better, they'll be rich the day they turn eighteen."

To her surprise, Ms. O'Grady said, "That's true, *if* they keep getting better. Trust me, Terri losing to you—not because you aren't good but because you're eleven—unnerved some people over at Aces."

"You're still in touch with them?" Andi asked, happy to be given an opening for a key question.

Ms. O'Grady nodded. "Yes, we're all still talking. The truth is, losing the chance to sign you didn't help me in terms of a full-time job going forward, but they've told me if I turn up anyone else, they'd be willing to talk to me again. I doubt I'm going to find anyone who is as close to being a lock as you."

"What if you could turn me up?" Andi asked.

For a moment Ms. O'Grady said nothing. Andi wondered if she smelled a setup.

"Are you saying . . . ?"

"Only that I'm curious," Andi said. "I haven't even discussed it with my parents yet. I just wonder if you'd be willing to fill me in on details—the kind of contracts I might get, how much money would be involved, that sort of thing. If the money is anything like what the Porters described, I'd be a little bit crazy to not at least take it to my parents."

"Your parents are both lawyers," Ms. O'Grady said. "I can't imagine that they aren't quite comfortable financially."

"They are," Andi said, then added, "but I'm guessing

you had some kind of pitch prepared to get their attention, didn't you?"

She hoped she wasn't pushing too hard, but Ms. O'Grady smiled. "You're a smart kid, Andi."

She paused just as the five-minute bell for first period rang.

"Your match tomorrow is at home, right?" she said. Knowing the answer was yes she said, "Why don't you tell your parents to pick you up a few minutes late and then come here afterward? I'll have something for you then."

Andi was tempted to ask if there would be something she could *show* her parents but decided not to appear too eager.

"Sounds fair," she said, standing up and extending her hand. "Thanks, Ms. O'Grady."

"No, Andi," the teacher said standing up, too. "Thank *you*."

Looking at the wide smile on Ms. O'Grady's face, a thought ran through Andi's mind: *Gotcha.*

She turned and walked out the door just as some of Ms. O'Grady's students were walking in.

The match the next day against Philadelphia West wasn't a walkover, but it was an easy win for Merion. The Mustangs had swept all eight matches in their first meeting with the Speedkids in the match played on the Penn campus.

The closest of those matches had been the number one boys' match between Gary Morrissey and Mike Jensen. Gary had come from behind in the third set to win 7–5, clinching the Merion sweep. Now it would be Jeff playing Jensen in the number one boys' slot.

It wasn't surprising that the Philly West kids came out swinging—literally and figuratively. They'd been embarrassed by the outcome of the first match and were 5–5 in the conference, proof that they were better than they had shown that day.

It was a surprisingly cool day for late April and Jeff had trouble getting loose. Before he could even think to take his sweater off, he was down 4–0 in the first set. Points weren't lasting very long—one reason Jeff couldn't get loose—because Jensen was blasting the ball off his forehand and his backhand and not missing very often.

Jeff finally held serve—and took his sweater off—to close to 4–1, but Jensen easily served out the set, winning 6–2.

Jeff glanced to the court next to his and saw that the first set of Andi's match had also ended 6–2. The difference was that Andi had the six.

Struggling to stay focused, Jeff quickly lost his serve to start the second set. During the changeover, he sat staring at the trees that surrounded the courts. Was this how his season was going to end? Losing to the best player for an inferior team and then having to face Tyler Porter in the finale? A little chill went through Jeff and he honestly wasn't sure if it was the wind or his current circumstance.

He decided he needed to change tactics. After all, what was there to lose? Instead of staying back and waiting for Jensen to blast another winner, he would attack—on everything. If Jensen passed him consistently, the match would be over quickly. If nothing else, he figured if he was going to lose, he might as well get it over with.

On the opening point of the next game, Jensen hammered a first serve down the middle. Jeff barely got his racquet on the ball, chipping it back to mid-court where Jensen could easily line up a blast off either wing.

But when the Speedkid saw Jeff charging the net, he took his eye off the ball and plopped a forehand into the net. He missed a first serve, spun a second serve to Jeff's backhand, and watched in surprise as Jeff slammed the ball crosscourt, came in, and easily put away the floater that came back at him.

Flustered, Jensen double-faulted. Then, Jeff crushed another second serve for a winner to win the game at love.

Holy Roger Federer!

Slowly but surely, Jensen adapted to Jeff's tactic, making him pay on occasion for his aggressiveness. But a lot of the confidence he'd had in the first set seemed to disappear. Feeling the pressure of Jeff's returns, his serve turned shaky. Jeff broke him to lead 4–2 and served out the set, coming in behind every single serve. When Jensen won a point with a perfect forehand blast down the line, he shook his fist and said, "That's it, that's the way you beat him!" On the next point, he tried the same shot and, with Jeff shading that way, hit it wide. Jeff won the set, 6–3.

By the time they reached 2–all in the third set, it had started to rain. Jeff had just hit a perfect drop volley to make it love–30 when he heard a loud whistle. Then came Coach Foster's voice: "Clear the courts, everyone," he shouted. "Lightning in the area. Everyone inside."

Jeff groaned. He knew there was no choice. If the school's lightning meter showed lightning anywhere close to where they were, they had to stop play for at least thirty minutes.

Andi was waiting when Jeff came off the court.

"Bad timing," she said. "I think you had control of the match."

"I assume you won?" he said.

"Yeah, I did, 2 and 2," she said. "We won all three girls' singles matches and Schnabel won his match."

"What about Gary?"

"Like you," she said. "Split sets and he's up 3–1 in the third."

"So, not exactly like me," he said. "He's up a break."

She shook her head. "Two breaks. He's serving at 3–1."

That meant the only match that was really in any doubt was Jeff's. Gary winning would clinch the match for Merion. Jeff saw the coaches from both teams consulting. Coach Foster walked over to where all the players had assembled, waiting for instructions. There was no sign at that moment of any lightning or thunder.

"We've decided to give it the required thirty minutes," he said. "If there are no further warnings in that time, we can start again and try to finish. If there is another warning, we'll have to call it off and the final score will be 4–0. Any questions?"

There were none. It was raining harder. Coach Foster noticed.

"Okay then, let's get inside. We can wait it out in the common area between the locker rooms. Merion kids, bring some towels from the locker rooms for the Philly West kids."

No one argued. They all sprinted to get inside. As soon as they were inside, Andi, who had a towel around her shoulders, grabbed Jeff's arm.

"I'm going upstairs to find Ms. O'Grady," she said.

She pulled her phone and her sweater from her racquet bag. "I've got my phone. If something happens, text me and I'll get right back down here."

"You aren't going to have to play again today, regardless," he said. "No way this goes to mixed."

She nodded. "I know. But whenever it's over or called, I don't want anyone asking where I went."

"Good luck," he said.

She smiled. "Let's hope I don't need it."

Andi turned and headed for the steps.

29

JOAN O'GRADY WAS STARING AT HER PHONE WHEN ANDI
walked into the room. The former coach smiled when
she saw it was her.

"They call it?" Ms. O'Grady asked.

"Not yet," Andi answered. "They're going to wait
thirty minutes, see if the lightning threat passes."

"You win your match already?"

Andi nodded. "Yes. We're up 4–0. Gary's up two
breaks in the third set of his match and Jeff's 2–all
but up love–30."

"So, finishing is really more about individual records than anything else."

"Right. But if they can finish . . ."

"They'd like to finish. I get it. Either way, you're
done for the day."

"Right," Andi said.

"Have a seat," Ms. O'Grady said, gesturing to a chair Andi guessed she had pulled next to her desk in anticipation of her arrival.

For a moment, Ms. O'Grady said nothing, looking directly at Andi as if she was trying to make a decision. For a split second Andi was reminded of what the French called the tiebreak: "jeu-decision"—the second word pronounced day-seesyon. It meant "game of decision," which Andi thought sounded a lot cooler than "tiebreak."

"So," Ms. O'Grady finally said, bringing Andi out of her French Open reverie, "have you spoken to your parents yet?"

Andi shook her head, sticking to the script. "I really think it would be better if I present everything to them at once. There's not much point in me saying, 'I'd like to see what Ms. O'Grady's proposing' without having anything to show them. At best, they say, 'Okay, ask Ms. O'Grady what would be involved.' At worst, they say, 'Absolutely not,' without even knowing what this might be about."

Ms. O'Grady nodded. "Like I said the other day, you're a very smart kid, Andi," she said. "That makes absolute sense. But let me ask you this: Are you *sure* you want to go ahead with this?"

Andi shook her head. "No, I'm not sure at all. I don't think I know enough to be sure. But the Porter twins did make me curious."

Ms. O'Grady went back to saying nothing. Finally, she reached into the drawer of her desk and pulled out a red-and-white folder that said *Aces Inc.* in gold lettering across the top. She looked at it for a moment, then handed it to Andi.

"Your parents are lawyers, so they'll be able to decipher the legalese in here," she said. "A lot of it—most of it—is boilerplate. The key areas for you and for them are the places where guaranteed money is mentioned. The bonus money or incentive money is just that, dependent on how well you play. It may be fun to read, but the truth is it doesn't mean that much right now."

Andi took the folder, then asked, "What's boilerplate?"

Ms. O'Grady smiled. "It's language that is standard in a contract. If you were to look at the Porters' contracts, a lot of it would be exactly the same as what's in there. You'd find it in all our junior contracts. The numbers in there are more important than the words."

Andi opened the folder and noticed instantly that the contract was between "Aces Inc. and Anthony and Jeannie Carillo."

Either following her eyes or reading her mind, Ms. O'Grady said, "The contract is between Aces and your parents for two reasons. First, as a minor, you can't sign a contract like this. Second, since none of the money is going directly to you, your amateur status isn't affected."

The Porters had already briefed her on that. Andi nodded and kept reading, following Ms. O'Grady's advice to skip over the words and get to the numbers. The first ones came on page three: "Company"—that was Aces—"agrees to pay Client $100,000 a year for first three years. Company then has option to continue contract for two more years at $200,000 per year."

Even without a law degree, Andi understood that Aces was saying *it* would decide if it wanted to keep Andi under contract after the first three years. The Carillos would not have the option to leave for five years; Aces could opt out after three. She started to point out the unfairness of such a setup but then, realizing this was a contract that would never be signed, she stopped.

She kept reading. The contract was eleven pages in all, but she got through it quickly, pausing only to read numbers: Income from any corporate contract—shoes, clothes, racquet, tennis club, etc.—would be an 80-20 split; the Carillos getting 80 percent. There was more about speaking opportunities (*Seriously?* Andi thought) and clinics.

"Wow," she said when she got to the end, noticing

the contract had spots for her parents to sign, as well as someone from Aces. "This is a lot of money—potentially."

"Like I said, the guaranteed money is what matters," Ms. O'Grady said. "But I think it's fair to say you *will* get contracts for things like your racquet, shoes, clothes. Corporate America likes young and attractive. You're both."

Andi decided this wasn't the moment to talk about how disgusting it was that an athlete's looks mattered so much. That was for another day in another setting.

"Any thoughts?" Ms. O'Grady asked as Andi's cell phone beeped to let her know a text was coming in.

It was from Jeff. *They're calling it. Better get down here.*

Andi held up the phone and told Ms. O'Grady what was in it. "This is definitely worth showing to my parents," she said—not lying, but leaving out that she would also be showing it to Jeff, his dad, and Stevie Thomas. She pushed the contract back into the folder.

"Let me know what they think," Ms. O'Grady said. "If they're interested, we can set up a meeting at our office to go over this in more detail." She smiled. "You don't even have to be there unless you want to be there."

"I'll be in touch," Andi said, heading for the door. She wasn't lying about that either.

Andi could see lightning in the distance as she looked out the windows on her way downstairs. She walked into the break area just as Coach Foster was starting to talk. "As you can tell, everyone, there's lightning in the area and it's still pouring," he said. He paused as Andi was trying to slip into a seat in the back row.

"Glad you could join us, Andi," he said, causing heads to turn and everyone to giggle a little. Andi decided no response was the best response.

Coach Foster seemed to agree. "Given the score, we've decided not to try to reschedule since this is the last week of the season. So, we're going to call it a 4–0 win for Merion." He turned in the direction of the two adults wearing jackets that said PHILLY WEST on them and said, "Coaches Baxter and Wilbern are agreed on this. I'm sorry for everyone that we didn't get to finish but God works in mysterious ways."

Andi was tempted to ask what was so mysterious about a thunderstorm but kept it to herself. Everyone stood up and handshakes were exchanged. As the Philly West players and coaches walked to the door, Jeff found Andi.

"So?" he said.

She had almost forgotten the red-and-white folder in her hands. Now she held it up. "Got it," she said. "It's all in here. I mean it's *all* in here."

Jeff's mouth dropped open. "Just like that—she turned it over to you just like that?"

"I think they want me pretty badly," she said.

"I think you should be nominated for an Academy Award," Jeff said.

Andi didn't disagree with that. She knew she'd done her job well.

"Now what?" she said.

Jeff was prepared. "You text Stevie and your parents. I'll text my dad. They can pick us up and we can go somewhere, look at this, and decide what's next."

Andi shook her head. "They're both working, remember? It's okay, though. We can talk to your dad and Stevie and then I'll update them when I get home."

"Perfect," Jeff said.

Andi felt a tingle go through her. She was excited. Also, nervous. It occurred to her they were playing for real now. There would be no *jeu-decision*. The games were over.

30

TOM MICHAELS AND STEVIE THOMAS ARRIVED IN ONE CAR
and they drove to a nearby McDonald's, not the one
at the mall but one just off I-95. At five o'clock, in the
middle of a downpour, it was relatively empty. Most
of those who did want food were using the drive-thru.

Now, they found an empty booth near the back of
the restaurant and sat down. Tom Michaels suggested
Andi not open the folder until they had all finished
eating, the better to avoid getting food on the documents. "We'll make copies," he said. "But let's keep
what we've got as clean as possible."

Everyone agreed and Andi put the folder on the
seat next to her while they all dug into their food. Jeff
appeared to be swallowing his food whole. He was
clearly starving and, as he'd said during the car ride,
still a little bit frustrated he hadn't gotten the chance

to finish his match with Mike Jensen. Andi was hungry, too. She ordered two hamburgers, French fries, and a vanilla milkshake.

"I had him," Jeff said more than once.

"Count it as a win then," his dad said.

That didn't seem to satisfy Jeff.

"Saying I had him is a lot different than saying I won," he said. "I played well, I'm happy about that. But, come on, Dad, you know it's not a win unless you actually win."

His dad smiled. "I get it but look at the glass as half full."

Andi had been finishing her second hamburger while the Michaelses argued about the definition of a win. Finishing up, she said, "Let's clear the table so you guys can look at what I've got."

They followed her instructions and, once the table was cleared, she pulled the contract out of the folder and showed them the highlights, pointing to the pages where specific dollar figures were mentioned.

"It's pretty funny they call it an 80-20 split," Jeff said. "Seems like 20 percent is a pretty hefty fee."

"It's standard," Stevie said as Jeff's dad nodded in agreement. "I wonder how much money the Porter twins were guaranteed."

"Remember, this is just an opening offer," Tom Michaels said. "They know they're going to be dealing with two lawyers. For example, I can't believe they think they're going to get away with a one-way option. They probably put it in there just so they can say, 'okay, we'll give you that one,' in return for something else."

"None of that's important," Andi said. "This isn't a negotiation. Stevie, you said we needed documents. Well, now we've got them."

Stevie nodded. "But Tom's right. We need to get our hands on the Porter contracts. Two sources, or three, are a lot better than one."

Jeff remembered something Andi had told him right after the Villanova match. "Didn't Tyler Porter say something to you about the fact that their dad had 'shopped' them to various agents?" he said.

"Yes," Andi said. "He was trying to tell me how into it their dad has been since they first showed potential."

"We need to find out who the other shoppers were. Then, we let them know Andi has an offer from Aces— my guess is it'll be on the agents' grapevine soon anyway—and tell them we're curious what the Porters were offered."

"While hinting that Andi might be open to other offers," Stevie added.

"Yes, exactly," Jeff said.

"I think before I call Renee Stubing back to set up an on-camera with her, you or your parents need to reach out to her," Mr. Michaels said. "Chances are good she'll have heard you're interested in possibly signing with someone. And, if she hasn't, you show her the contract."

Andi nodded. "I'll text her tonight," she said.

"And I'll take the contract into my office tonight and make copies," Mr. Michaels said.

"Sooner the better," Stevie said.

They stopped at the counter on the way out so Stevie and Mr. Michaels could get coffee. Jeff got an apple pie. Andi got nothing. She was full and fired up.

Even though she was eager to send Renee Stubing the "bait" text as Mr. Michaels had called it, Andi decided to do two things first: her homework and a sit-down to update her parents.

They both agreed that outing the agents as subhuman predators was a good idea but were a little concerned about how they would respond if Stevie wrote the story and Tom Michaels put it on NBC Sports–Philadelphia.

"What do you mean?" Andi said.

"I mean, who knows how many kids have contracts involving their parents getting paid for their services?" Andi's mom said. "What if the people who run women's tennis investigate? Or kids are declared ineligible to play in high school or college? That could make a lot of people unhappy."

"The point is to make the agents unhappy," Andi said. "And to get them to stop preying on kids like me and the Porter twins. I'm lucky because I have parents like you who would never get involved in this sort of thing. I have a feeling I might be in the minority."

Her dad sighed. "Sadly, I think you're probably right," he said. "See what Stubing says. If she agrees to meet, I think one of us should go with you."

Andi shook her head. "I'm a lot less threatening than you guys and your law degrees," she said. "Remember, we want her to feel confident—over-confident if at all possible."

Andi had left her cell phone sitting on her bed when she'd gone downstairs to talk to her parents. She picked it up and was about to look up Renee Stubing's number, when she saw she had two new texts. One, predictably, was from Jeff: *What did your parents say?*

The second one was from Renee Stubing. Andi almost burst out laughing when she saw it. She wondered for a second if Stubing was bugging the house. Then she read the text: *Word on the street is that u are reconsidering yr initial position. Understand Aces is making u an offer. PLEASE dont sign anything before talking to me—in person. Bring yr parents if you want.*

Andi was tempted to show the text to her parents before responding. She realized that was redundant: they had already agreed Andi should meet Stubing. Her text just made it easier.

OK, she wrote. *Aces has MADE an offer. Looks pretty good. Where? When?*

She didn't have to wait long for an answer. *Tomorrow after u practice? If ur parents are coming, we can all meet at Mario's—very good Italian, close to your school.*

Just me, Andi texted back. *Can you pick me up at 5:30?*

C u then, was Stubing's last response—her words followed by a smiley face. Andi rolled her eyes and sat back on her bed. That had been easy. But was it too easy?

By the time Andi and her dad got in the car for school the next morning she had yet another text—this one from Tad Walters. It said roughly the same thing as Stubing's text the night before. *Since you've already met with Aces, how about we talk on Wednesday after you practice?*

Andi already had her meeting with Stubing set for Wednesday. *Big test on Thursday*, she wrote—a flat-out lie. *I could do it Thursday after practice as long as we finish at a reasonable hour. Fairly important match on Friday!*

LOL, no kidding on the match. Thursday's fine—as long as you promise not to sign with anyone else before then!

When Andi showed Walters's texts to her dad, he smiled and said, "I thought there was no honor among thieves in the legal business. This is beyond that."

"Isn't putting honor with thieves in the same sentence an oxymoron?" Andi answered.

He shook his head. "You're eleven and you know what an oxymoron is?" he said.

"It was a spelling word in fourth grade, Dad," Andi said.

Her father sighed. "I really am getting old," he said with a laugh.

It wasn't until lunchtime that Andi had a chance to fill Jeff in on the details of her text swaps with Stubing and Walters. Maria Medley, Eleanor Dove, and Danny Diskin were sitting with them when Andi brought everyone up to date.

"Guess it pays to be pretty and white," Maria said with her usual devilish grin.

Danny, who was also Black, pointed at Maria and said, "Doesn't hurt to be talented, either, does it?" he said. "You're just jealous."

"Darn right I'm jealous. It'll be ten more years before I can cash in on being a great basketball player."

"You better take some pills to make you taller," Eleanor said. "I don't see a lot of five-one point guards in the WNBA."

"Better to be five-one than six-one," Maria said.

"I'm six feet, not six-one," Eleanor said. "And in basketball, you're darn right it's better to be six-one than five-one."

Danny, who was unofficially Eleanor's boyfriend, said, "I thought you told me you were five-thirteen."

"Shut up, squirt," Eleanor said. Danny was five-nine but built like a block of ice. No one in the school would think of messing with him. Jeff, who had to stretch to be five-six, wouldn't think of messing with Eleanor, Danny or, for that matter, Maria. Much as he enjoyed the verbal skirmish, he wanted to get back to Andi and her meeting that day with Stubing.

"You should wear a wire," he said.

"What is this, *Blue Bloods*?" Andi said, a reference to a cop show they had all watched in the past.

"You could just turn on your cell phone's voice recorder," Danny said.

Andi shook her head. "I've got a better idea. I'll be up front. I'll tell her I'm going to bring the contract offered by Aces so she can see I'm not bluffing about the numbers, but I need to see her numbers in writing to show my parents."

"You think she'll go for that?" Maria said. "I wouldn't."

"This woman thinks she's the smartest guy in every room she walks into," Andi said. "She'll go for it."

"I think you're right," Jeff said. "I'd text her right now. If you wait till after school, she might claim she doesn't have time to put it together."

Andi thought this made sense. "See you at practice," she said to Jeff. "See the rest of you later."

"Hey, keep us informed," Maria shouted after her as she started to walk away.

Andi kept walking. "Jeff, if you don't let us know what's going on, Danny's going to beat you up," Maria said.

"I'm not at all afraid of Danny," Jeff said. "*You* scare me."

31

PRACTICE ON WEDNESDAY WAS ROUTINE. TUESDAY'S RAIN was gone and as often happened in spring in Philadelphia, the weather had gone from miserable to beautiful overnight.

The coaches had Jeff and Andi play mixed doubles against Gary and Lisa the last thirty minutes of the practice, the idea being that there was a decent chance that mixed doubles would decide Friday's match.

The only way for Merion to win the conference championship outright was to win the match by at least 5–3. That would mean the two teams were both 11–1 and Merion would win the tiebreak because the overall score for the two matches between the schools would be 9–8 in Merion's favor. If Merion won 5–4, it had been decided that week that a one-set tiebreaker would be played. The coaches would decide who would play the tiebreak: boys' singles; girls' singles, or mixed doubles. If the set reached 6–all, whoever was playing would decide the entire season in a tiebreak. Talk about "jeu-decision."

Coach Foster walked through the potential scenarios. "Bottom line is we worry about winning the match—period," he said. "The rest will take care of itself one way or the other."

Jeff wasn't sure how to feel. On the one hand, he was dying to play with Andi against the Porter twins in mixed doubles. On the other hand, he wasn't sure he wanted to potentially have to play one set with the entire season at stake against Tyler Porter. He knew his game had improved considerably throughout the spring—the daily practices certainly helped but so did playing with Andi on most Saturdays. His dad always said the best way to improve at any sport was to play up—compete with people who are better than you. Andi had given him the chance to play up.

When practice was over, Jeff checked with Andi before everyone headed inside to shower.

"You still up for this?" he asked.

They were both sweating in the heat after the half hour of mixed doubles. Lisa and Gary were a good combination, and the coaches had stopped the set with Jeff and Andi up a break at 4–3. Lisa's height made her very effective at the net and Gary was solid from the backcourt. It had been a good workout.

"More than up for it," Andi answered. "She's picking me up in twenty minutes." She smiled. "I've never been to Mario's, but my parents say it's very good."

"You sound like me—the food's more important than the meeting."

She smiled. "You're right," she said. "Don't worry. I'm up for the meeting."

"Text me . . ."

She put up a hand. "You know I will," she said as she turned and headed inside to shower.

Renee Stubing was waiting for Andi at the circle when she walked outside at exactly 5:30. She'd actually been ready a couple minutes earlier but didn't want to show up before the appointed time and look too eager. Stubing was driving a sporty red BMW convertible, although she had the top up.

"Trust me you'll be more comfortable with the top up when we get on I-95," she said, reading Andi's mind as she climbed in.

"We're going on I-95?" Andi said.

"Just for a couple miles," she said. "The restaurant is in Conshohocken."

They made small talk during the ride, Renee asking about Friday's match and how school was going.

"Do you date Jeff Michaels?" she asked as they pulled onto the interstate.

"Date?" Andi said. "We're eleven years old."

Stubing shrugged. "I had my first boyfriend in fifth grade."

"But you're not married, right?" Andi said.

"Nope. And very happy," she answered.

Before long, they pulled into what appeared to be a crowded parking lot.

"Don't worry," Stubing said, again reading Andi's mind as they climbed out of the car. "I know the owner. We've got a table waiting for us."

It wasn't just a table, it was a room, one that was obviously used for private parties. "I thought privacy and quiet would make things easier for both of us," Stubing said. "That's why I chose this place. Mario's a friend. Plus, like I said, the food's really good."

"So the owner's name really is Mario?" Andi said as they were seated.

"Yup. He'll come by in a little while."

They ordered drinks—white wine for Renee, Coke for Andi. Sure enough, as promised, Mario showed up with their drinks. He was young for someone who owned a restaurant and he and Renee exchanged enthusiastic greetings. When Renee introduced Mario to Andi, he lavishly bent over to kiss her hand.

Then came the pitch.

"I know who you are, Ms. Carillo," he said. "I've seen you on TV dating to your soccer season and I'm very much a fan. I didn't know until Renee told me what a tennis prodigy you are. Is there any sport in which you aren't gifted?"

He was clearly from Philadelphia. The word *very* came out "vurry," and Andi could hear the accent throughout his monologue.

Andi smiled and thanked him. He then told them that once the waitress delivered the menu, if there was anything not on it that they wanted, to just order it and he would make it for them.

They thanked him and, after looking at the menu, Andi decided to order veal pizzaiola, a dish her mother liked to fix. She asked for spaghetti with red sauce on the side. That would be plenty of food. Renee ordered some kind of fish. She ordered it in Italian.

"You speak Italian?" Andi said.

"Enough to get by in restaurants in Italy," she said. "That's about it."

It was time, Andi thought, *to get down to business*. Again, Renee seemed to know what she was thinking. Andi was beginning to worry she also knew the real purpose of the meeting.

"So," she said. "You said you had an offer from Aces."

Andi had carried her backpack into the restaurant. She reached down, opened it, and pulled the Aces contract out and slid it across the table to Renee.

Renee took her time reading through it even though only the paragraphs with numbers in them were relevant. She finished, carefully put the contract back in the folder Andi had put it in, and handed it back to Andi.

"That's an impressive offer," she said. She glanced at Andi's phone, which was sitting on the table next to her. "You aren't recording, are you?"

Andi handed her the phone so she could see for herself. Stevie's instinct about not trying to record the conversation had been right. Renee smiled and handed it back.

"Sorry," she said. "Agent's paranoia."

"I thought you told me you weren't an agent," Andi said.

Renee smiled. "You're right, I did—and I'm not in the traditional sense. I never tried to recruit you until I heard you had told the Aces people you were willing to listen to them."

"I'm curious," Andi asked. "How *did* you hear I was talking to them?"

Renee smiled. "In this business there are no secrets."

"You mean the agent business," Andi said.

"Touché," Renee said and they both laughed.

"So, should I sign with Aces?" Andi asked.

Renee shrugged. "You can and you'll make a lot of money, regardless of how your career turns out. But you might want to take a look at this first."

She reached down to where her briefcase was under the table. She pulled it onto the empty chair next to her, opened it, picked out a file and handed it to Andi.

"This is an opening offer, just like the Aces contract is, I'm sure, an opening offer," she said. "This should show you how much we think of you." She paused and smiled. "Actually, how much *I* think of you. I've been watching you play since last summer."

Andi opened the file and paged through. It wasn't identical to the Aces contract but certainly similar. It named her parents as the clients and designated them as "outside legal counsel for tennis affairs" for New Advantage. That made sense for two lawyers not likely to be even semi-qualified to be junior talent scouts.

There was more detail about corporate appearances and how she would be placed in professional tournaments when she was fourteen—the youngest age a player could enter a professional event.

The bottom line, though, was the bottom line. The guaranteed money was double what Aces Inc. was offering; the money she would receive for signing corporate contracts was also considerably higher.

"Outside legal counsel for tennis affairs?" Andi said as she finished.

Renee shrugged. "They're a lot more qualified as lawyers than Earl Woods was as a golf junior talent scout for IMG, aren't they?"

"I don't know," Andi said with a smile. "Earl did produce a pretty good junior golfer for them, didn't he?"

Renee laughed.

"Show that to your parents," she said. "Then let me know what you think."

"I will," Andi promised as the waitress, with Mario right behind her, arrived with their food.

32

ANDI SHOWED THE NEW ADVANTAGE PROPOSAL TO HER parents as soon as she got home. While they looked through it, she called Jeff to update him.

"I'll tell my father," he said. "You call Stevie."

"We need to move quickly on this," Stevie said when Andi filled him in. "Once you meet with Walters tomorrow, we need to pull the story together right away—get it on the air and up on the *Inquirer* website and in the Sunday paper—latest."

"What's the rush?" Andi asked.

"What did Stubing say to you about nothing staying secret in the agent world? I guarantee you they'll all be at the match Friday—remember Aces represents the Porters, so they'll be there for sure. They start talking and next thing you know they'll come up with some kind of joint denial."

"So?" Andi said. "We've got the documents, remember?"

Stevie laughed. "You're right, we do. But I promise you, they've all got media people who will print anything they tell them to print—or say on TV. You ever watch Golf Channel or Tennis Channel? They're both apologists for everyone in their sport and they reach a lot of people."

Andi was almost certain that he was right. "So, it sounds like we all need to get together tomorrow after I meet with Walters."

Stevie agreed.

Andi called Jeff, who said he would talk to his father. She went downstairs and found her parents sitting at the kitchen table. Her father was holding the New Advantage proposed contract in his hands.

"The money proposed here is *incredible*," he said, shaking his head. "A lot of it is tied to how well you play, but the guaranteed money alone would put you through college and law school—with plenty to spare."

"Dad, you're not thinking . . ."

"Of course not," he said, laughing. "I remember reading a book years ago that made the case that tennis eats its young—especially the girls. Here's proof." He smiled. "But did you like the law school idea?"

Andi laughed. Then she filled her parents in on what Stevie had said. She was just finishing when the home phone rang. Her mother answered. "Hang on, Tom, let me put you on speaker," she said.

"I've got Jeff with me and Stevie's conferenced in," Tom Michaels said. "We're in agreement we should meet tomorrow and get this story out in public over the weekend. Question is, where to meet?"

Andi's first thought was Mario's—the food *had* been really good—and there was the private room where she and Stubing had eaten. Then again, Mario was too close to Stubing for comfort. There was also Andy's, but that was much too public a place.

It was Jeff who spoke up first. "Dad, what about your office? There's that big meeting room in the back and no one's playing tomorrow, so getting there won't be a problem."

"That could work," Tom Michaels said. "Flyers and Sixers are off tomorrow, and the Phillies are in Cincinnati. You guys mind driving to south Philly?"

The NBC Sports–Philadelphia studio was actually inside the Wells Fargo Center—the arena where the Sixers and Flyers played. On a game night, getting into the parking lot could be an issue. But with no game going on, it would be fine.

Everyone agreed that would work.

"I'll have some pizzas sent in by Celebres," Tom Michaels said. "If we meet at seven, is that enough time for you guys to get there after Andi's meeting?"

"Should be okay," Andi's dad said. "Unless we hit some kind of traffic coming around 95."

"Good luck, Andi," Stevie said, clearly referencing the Walters meeting.

"Good luck to us all," Andi answered.

33

TAD WALTERS ALSO SUGGESTED ITALIAN, A PLACE CALLED Tony's that wasn't nearly as fancy as Mario's. In fact, it was clearly a pizza place with a few other items on the menu as opposed to the other way around. There was no veal pizzaiola.

Since Jeff had told her that the pizza from Celebres was every bit as good as Andy's, Andi ordered a small plate of pasta with marinara sauce and limited herself to one piece of the bread—which was quite good.

Walters had arrived at the circle after practice with a woman who reminded Andi a little—maybe a lot—of Renee Stubing. Young, blond, and, when she got out of the car at the restaurant, quite tall. Clearly, Andi thought, an ex-player.

She introduced herself as Monica Alston and

Walters quickly explained why she was along. "If you sign with us, Monica will be your representative," he said. "She played on the circuit for several years and reps several players who are now in the top 100."

Andi thought it amusing that agents never used the word 'agent,' to describe themselves.

Surprisingly, Alston shook her head at Walters's lavish introduction. "I played in a grand total of four WTA events," she said, almost echoing Joan O'Grady's description of her career. "All four times I got wild cards into the event. I *did* spend five years on the Futures circuit, which is the minor leagues of women's tennis, so I understand something about the struggle. I *do* represent five top 100 players."

"Who's your highest ranked player?" Andi asked.

"Tracy Gordon," Alston said.

Andi had never heard the name. "What's she ranked?" she asked.

"Fifty-seventh," Alston answered.

"With a bullet," Walters added quickly. A bullet meant you were on the way up.

The two non-agents made small talk until Walters pulled into the restaurant's parking lot. Practice had ended—as planned—early because the coaches didn't want the team leaving its energy on the practice court. It was 5:20 when they arrived and plenty of tables available. They grabbed a booth in the back.

Once they had ordered, it was Alston who took control of the meeting.

"We understand you've met with both Aces and New Advantage to talk about representation," she said.

"I have," Andi nodded. "They both put offers in writing in front of me."

"We can top whatever they've offered," Walters said, causing Alston to shoot him what was clearly a "keep quiet" look. Andi remembered what Tom Ross had told her father: Walters was known as a keen judge of talent. Clearly, though, when it came to negotiation, he wasn't the brightest bulb in the room.

"I want you to know that Renee's a friend," Alston said. "We both played the Futures tour together for a couple of years. She's a good person and very good at her job."

Andi's thought was simple: Yes, good at her job. Not so much the good person part.

Alston continued. "I'm sure you've googled all three groups. If you have, you know ProStyles has the longest history and we have more contacts in other sports than either of the other two. New Advantage has some, Aces has none.

"How is that relevant?" Andi asked.

"We cross-market a lot," Alston said. "We can put you in campaigns with players from the WNBA or the

NBA for that matter. We just signed Chip Graber, you know who he is, right?"

Andi did. Graber was the starting point guard for the Minnesota Timberwolves. He'd been on the Olympic team and was a marketing phenomenon because he was a good-looking guy.

Andi nodded that she knew Graber. "Well, we just signed him. Would you like to be in a commercial with him someday?"

Andi remembered she was playing a game here so she decided not to ask how a teenaged tennis player and a thirty-ish basketball player (Graber would be at least that old by the time Andi turned fourteen) would pair up in a commercial. Instead, she just said, "That sounds pretty cool."

"There's lots more that's cool," Alston continued.

Andi waited several beats before answering. "As my father likes to say, 'You've got my attention,'" she said. "Do you have an offer of some kind?"

The food arrived. Alston pulled a contract from her briefcase and put it on the open space next to where Andi was sitting. "Read it when you're finished eating," she said.

Andi made a point of not rushing through her food. She didn't want to eat too much or too quickly both for strategic reasons and to be sure she had room for the pizza later.

When she'd finished about half of the pasta, she pushed it to the side and turned her attention to the contract. "My parents will have to read this, you know that, right?" she said, playing the charade to the max.

"Of course. They're the ones who will have to sign it and they're the ones who've dealt with legal documents," Alston said with a smile. "I've circled the places that are easy to understand—and most important."

Andi looked through the document. It wasn't that different from the other two contracts. The guarantee numbers were closer to Aces than New Advantage, but the incentive dollars—corporate deals, marketing— were considerably higher. She wanted to stick the contract in her backpack and bolt—she had everything she needed. But she had to play the game to the finish.

"So, the guarantee number is payable whenever we sign right?" she asked. "These other numbers don't kick in until I'm eligible to play in pro tournaments."

Alston nodded. "And would be dependent, of course, on your success. But that first number is yours if you never win a match."

Andi wanted to say, "Duh, I know what the word guaranteed means," but refrained.

She asked a few more meaningless questions. The waiter returned to ask if anyone wanted dessert. "I've got to get going," she said. "I've got homework to do and the match tomorrow."

"We'll be there!" Walters said enthusiastically. Of all the non-agents Andi had dealt with in the last two months, he was easily the smarmiest.

Alston asked the waiter for the check. It was a twenty-minute drive back to the Carillos' house. When they pulled into the driveway, Alston got out of the car and shook Andi's hand one more time.

"No matter who you sign with, Andi, you'll be fine. The guarantees are found money for your family. But I think if you and your parents do some homework, you'll find our track record is miles ahead of the other guys. They know what they're doing, don't get me wrong, we just have more experience and more contacts."

Andi nodded, not wanting to extend the conversation. "I'll talk to my parents," she said—telling the absolute truth.

Alston gave her a thumbs-up and said, "Good luck tomorrow."

With that she got into the car. Andi walked into the house. The good news was she'd finished her homework in study hall. Now, the real work could begin.

The Carillos walked in the door at NBC Sports–Philadelphia at 7:05.

"They're all waiting for you in the conference room," the guard said. "Come on, I'll show you."

He walked them in and pointed through the newsroom. "Go all the way back and turn left," he said. "You'll run right into it."

There were five pizza boxes sitting on the conference table when they walked in and Andi almost laughed out loud seeing both Jeff and Stevie devouring slices.

"We thought we'd all eat first, then work," Tom Michaels said, seeing the amused/bemused looks on the faces of the three Carillos.

Jeff hadn't been kidding about Celebres pizza. Even after eating the pasta at Tony's, Andi easily put away two slices and was thinking about a third when Mr. Michaels said, "Everyone ready to get to work?"

Everyone was still eating, but also ready to get started—especially Andi and, no doubt, Jeff, who had their minds on the next day's match.

Andi had handed the ProStyles contract to Mr. Michaels when they first walked in the door and he'd gone out to get someone to make copies for everyone. When the young man who'd made the copies walked back in with them, Mr. Michaels handed one to everyone.

"So," he said with a smile. "We have now officially carried out the Bob Woodward–Bobby Kelleher–Stevie Thomas mission of getting the documents." All six people in the room now had all three contracts in front of them.

Mr. Michaels turned to the Carillos. "Lawyers, any observations?"

It was Andi's dad who answered. That made sense. A lot of his job was negotiating and reading contracts, although he did work in courtrooms some of the time. Her mother was a full-time litigator, meaning she did most of her work in a courtroom, representing clients who either went before a judge or were involved in a trial.

"What's pretty clear here is that all these agencies have standard contracts with basically the same boilerplate language," he said. "The only thing that changes are the numbers."

"And that's important why?" Jeff asked.

"Because, Jeff, it makes it pretty clear that offering this kind of deal to kids who aren't even fourteen yet is something they do all the time."

"But technically they're not breaking any rules or laws, right?" Stevie asked.

"Absolutely not," Andi's dad said. "That's why there's absolutely no mention of you—Andi—in any of these. In each case, your parents are being hired for their legal expertise in some way and this is the money *we* will be paid. It's also why the wording on the incentive money says simply, 'Should a player be brought to the attention of the company by the new employees at any point, these are the dollar figures to be paid.' No specific mention of Andi anywhere. It's also especially clever because it means if, say, Andi convinced a talented friend to sign, there's that much more money on the table."

"So there are no laws being broken here or, in fact, any rules of the WTA, right?" Stevie asked.

Tony Carillo nodded. "No laws, no rules, unless you count rules of morality or decency. Asking an eleven-year-old kid to turn pro? It's disgusting."

"Which is what the story's about," Stevie said.

"That and the fact that this sort of thing is anything but new," Tom Michaels added. He turned back to the Carillos. "Tony, your friend Tom Ross is prepared to go on camera and say that?" he asked.

Tony Carillo smiled. "Yes, as long as we make it clear—or he's allowed to make it clear—that he only represents men and has never been involved in any of this. Also, he insists he has to be identified as a 'player representative,' not an agent.

"Of course he does," Tom Michaels said with a wry smile.

"So," Andi said, "what's next?"

Mr. Michaels and Stevie looked at each other. "It's time for us to do our jobs now that you've given us the documents we need. It's pretty much 100 percent guaranteed that they'll all be at the match tomorrow. I'll be there with a camera crew and Stevie will be there with a tape recorder. We'll go from there."

"So, tomorrow is the climax of everything," Jeff said.

Andi smiled at him. "Everything," she said. "You better be ready to play, partner."

34

FRIDAY DAWNED RAINY AND WARM, BUT THE WEATHER
report called for the skies to clear by noon. The temperature would be in the 80s when the match began.

Neither Andi nor Jeff was paying much attention
during their classes. Even lunch was quiet. There
wasn't much to say. Everyone at the table knew what
was at stake on the court that afternoon even though
Maria, Eleanor, and Danny didn't know the details of
what might be at stake off the court. Even Maria had
little to say. Danny pointed out that, especially since it
was a Friday, they could expect a large student turnout.

He wasn't kidding. In addition to all the kids from
Merion who came out to watch the match, Villanova
had brought several busloads of kids up the Main
Line to root their team to the title and an undefeated
season.

Even Tyler Porter noticed the size of the crowd as he and Jeff walked onto Court 1 to warm up. "I played in the Orange Bowl tournament for elite juniors and I never saw this many people at a match," he said. He smiled. "Should be fun, huh?"

Jeff wasn't sure how much fun it was going to be playing Porter. He was giving up two years, eight inches and—clearly—a ton of experience. And yet, he felt okay with it all because he knew all the pressure was on Porter. Even with the crowds as thick as they were, he could see Mr. Porter standing right up front, watching Tyler on Court 1 and Terri on Court 2. Jeff knew his parents were there, too—somewhere in the crowd—but he also knew they'd be proud of him regardless of outcome. It was a calming thought.

One court over, Andi *was* nervous. She wasn't thinking about parental pressure, but she knew that Tyler Porter was going to be a tough out for Jeff no matter how well he played. That meant she pretty much *had* to beat Terri because if Merion got down 2–0 it would be awfully hard for them to even get to a 4–4 split and create the need for a mixed doubles match.

Terri had been smiling and friendly during warm-ups but once the match began, she was all business. Andi liked that—it forced her to focus right away.

The first set went to a tiebreak. Andi wasn't surprised. With her height, Terri had an excellent serve and was tough to break. When Andi *did* break her to lead 4–3, she broke right back with two surprisingly good crosscourt backhands that Andi couldn't get to.

"Girl's good," Andi said under her breath. She stole a glance at court one: Jeff had lost the first set, 6–2. *Whoo boy*, she thought. *Dig in.*

She did just that during the tiebreak, getting every first serve in. Nerves seemed to get to Terri a little. She kept missing first serves and, with Andi up 5–4, she double-faulted, giving Andi set point. Not wanting to face a second serve on set point she twisted her first serve in without its usual power, making sure she got it in. Andi had guessed right that she would do that. She took the serve high and early and blasted it into the corner, just inside both the sideline and the baseline. Terri never moved, just put her racquet in the air and said, "good one."

Meanwhile, Jeff was fighting to get into his match. Tyler Porter missed several first serves at 2–all and Jeff managed to get a break. But, serving for the set at 5–4, *he* got nervous and Porter broke him back. On they went to 6–all and the tiebreak.

At the very least, Jeff wanted to force a third set. Clearly, Porter didn't want to play a third set. And there was his father, bellowing at him to, "End this now. Come on, Tyler, get this over and done with."

Jeff almost laughed. He was pretty certain the last

thing Tyler needed right now was his dad making him feel as if playing a third set would be a loss. Sure enough, Tyler began spraying shots, even missing a couple of easy put-away volleys. Down 6–2, he tried a drop shot that sat up so high that Jeff crushed it down the line to win the set.

As they changed sides, Jeff heard Mr. Porter again. Villanova's coach had come down—as was allowed—to talk to Tyler before the third set began. He was talking quietly to him, but Jeff doubted Tyler could hear much because his father was screaming again.

"Regroup, Tyler," he said. "Six–love now. Six–love. No reason for him to win another game."

Jeff was walking past Tyler and the coach to take the court when he heard the coach say softly, "Let me handle this, Tyler."

He saw that Tyler had turned in the direction of his father and was clearly about to say something. He stopped and the coach walked over to talk to the irate father.

The third set was over quickly, and it was almost 6–0—for Jeff. Tyler Porter played so poorly that Jeff wondered if he was tanking—the tennis term for trying to lose on purpose.

Jeff broke to start the set and then broke again to lead 3–0. Tyler hit every shot as hard as he could in the next game and Jeff never had to hit more than two shots to win a point. At 4–0, Tyler, serving every ball as hard as he could, served three aces to hold for 4–1. But that was it. Jeff could almost imagine dents in the fence from some of Tyler's shots slamming into it—on the fly. Bart Porter—Jeff had heard Tyler's coach call him by his first name—had gone completely silent.

When they shook hands at the net, Tyler said, "I'm really sorry. I didn't even give you a chance to earn the third set. I just lost it with my father."

"I don't blame you," Jeff said. "*I'm* really sorry."

He started to tell him he should calm himself down in case they had to play mixed doubles but decided against it. This was still about winning the match.

Terri Porter certainly didn't tank after losing the first set, but Andi was just a little too good for her. She broke her twice in the second set and nailed just about every first serve, which made it almost impossible for Porter to get close to breaking her serve. She served it out at 5–3 for a 7–6, 6–3 win.

Terri was completely gracious at the net. "I played well today, especially in the first set," she said. "You were just better. If I were an agent, I'd certainly be trying to get your name on a contract."

Andi smiled. "Well, I suspect there are several of them here right now who agree with you," she said.

Terri nodded. "Saw Renee Stubing and Joan O'Grady talking to each other before we walked on court."

Andi hadn't noticed any of the agents in the packed crowd but had no doubt they were there. After accepting congratulations from her parents, her teammates, and her coaches, she walked over to find a spot to watch Jeff play the third set against Tyler Porter. She was a little surprised, but very pleased, to see Jeff had taken Tyler to a third set. She hadn't expected that to happen.

That was the good news. The not-so-good news was that Gary Morrissey was about to lose the number two singles match on the boys' side and Lisa Carmichael was 2–all in the third in the number two girls' match. The number three girls' singles match had just taken over the court where she and Terri had been playing. Since there were only four courts, the boys' number three singles match and the doubles matches couldn't start until the other matches between the ones and twos were finished.

Jeff was up 2–0 and serving. Tyler Porter looked like he wanted to be anywhere except on a tennis court at that moment. He seemed to swing at every ball as if trying to hit it into the fence on a fly—which he did on several occasions—rather than landing it inside the lines of the court.

"Something happened with my dad," Terri Porter

said, walking up to stand next to Andi. "I could hear him shouting during the second set but couldn't hear what he was saying. Whatever it was, it got to Tyler. No offense to Jeff, but I think he's tanking."

"He *wants* to lose?" Andi said incredulously.

"Not so much wants to lose as wants to do something to make my dad angry. He's pushing back really hard about going to IMG in the fall. My dad told him this morning that he should win love-and-love against Jeff."

"Well, he's not going to do that," Andi said as the players changed sides with Jeff up 3–0.

Tyler Porter didn't even pause to use his towel to wipe the sweat off his face.

"Where's your dad?" Andi asked, not seeing him in the crowd.

"Probably left," Terri said. "He knew I could lose to you, but he's not happy about it, I promise you that. And now this . . ." She gestured at the court.

"What happens tonight, when you get home?" Andi asked.

"No idea," Terri said. "But it won't go well. Not well at all."

35

ANDI GAVE JEFF A BIG HUG COMING OFF THE COURT AFTER
his win over Tyler Porter. As it turned out, Lisa Carmichael had pulled out her match, but Gary Morrissey
had lost. Unfortunately, Villanova had won both of the
number three singles matches, meaning the match was
tied at three. About an hour later, the doubles matches
were split—Merion's girls' doubles team hadn't lost all
season. That meant the score was tied 4–4 and mixed
doubles would decide the outcome. Everyone knew
that if Merion won, the teams would both be 11–1 for
the season and would each have won nine individual
matches against the other.

The coaches would then have to make a final decision on who would play in order to break the tie for the
conference championship.

Either way, Jeff was fired up at the thought of perhaps playing with Andi one more time and making up for their loss to the Porters a few weeks earlier.

"Don't expect Tyler to give up now," Andi said as they walked on court with raucous cheers reigning down on all four players. "He isn't going to want to let his sister down."

Jeff suspected that was so but was very happy to see the Porters' dad back at his courtside station almost directly behind the players' changeover chairs. The closer he was to his kids the better it was for Jeff and Andi.

Andi had also spotted Mr. Porter. "The old man is back," she said with a slight nod of her head. "Good for us."

Andi was right about Tyler Porter being a different player than he had been in the final set of the singles. He seemed to nail every first serve. Fortunately, Jeff and Andi were both serving well, too, and they played the entire first set to 6–1 all without anyone losing their serve. Jeff suspected the tiebreak would be critical: If they could win it, something was bound to go out of the Porters, especially, he suspected, Tyler.

The only bad news was that Bart Porter had been noticeably silent throughout the set.

Tyler served first to start the tiebreak and promptly aced Andi. Jeff responded with two good serves of his own for a 2–1 lead. No one, it seemed, could even get a mini-break—one point—on the opponents' serve.

Jeff and Andi were up 6–5 with Terri serving at set point. She missed her first serve and Jeff attacked the second serve, hitting a flat forehand into the corner. Tyler ran it down and floated a weak backhand that Andi closed on for a put-away volley.

The ball was in the air when Jeff heard a voice yell, "OUT, IT WAS OUT! OUT!"

Andi followed through and then put the volley away. Everyone turned in the direction of the voice. It was Mr. Porter.

"That shot in the corner was out!" he screamed. "Everyone saw it! The score's 6–all. Go ahead and serve, Terri."

His children were staring at him, clearly not sure what to say. At this level of tennis, players called their own lines and most gave the benefit of the doubt to the opponent on any shot that was close. Jeff had known his return was in, both from the feel of the shot and from eyeballing it as Tyler tried to run it down. Clearly, the thought of it being out had never occurred to Tyler.

There was complete silence for a moment until Tyler said. "The ball was good, Dad—way good."

"NO, IT WASN'T!" his father shouted. "You can't always be the good guy, Tyler. Ball was out. Terri, serve!"

Terri wasn't anywhere close to serving. "They won

the set, Dad," she said, walking toward the chairs to change sides.

"NO, THEY DIDN'T!"

He gestured for Villanova's coaches, demanding they get involved. Seeing them walk onto the court, Coach Foster and Coach Wentworth followed them.

"Bart, I honestly couldn't see where the ball landed from where I was standing," one of the Villanova coaches said. He was wearing a button that said, 'Coach Ted Harrison, Villanova.' The coaches and players had all been given hastily made-up buttons to make it easier for them to get around at the start of the day. "But it was Tyler's call and he played the ball as good."

"I don't care!" Mr. Porter said. "He always does that. He'd rather be a nice guy than a winner. You know that, Ted. Now, are you going to stand up for your players or not?"

"He *is* standing up for his player," Coach Foster said, jumping in. "His player wants to play the match fair and square and you're trying to prevent that."

Coach Foster's voice was raised, and he was about as emotional as Jeff had seen him all season. Mr. Porter was standing, hands on hips, staring at Coach Harrison. The Villanova coach looked at Coach Foster almost pleadingly. "Bill, how would you feel about playing a let—" which in tennis-speak meant playing the point over.

Before Coach Foster could answer, Tyler Porter did. "Oh no, not happening. The ball wasn't close to being out. They won the set fair-and-square."

"Tyler, you do what I'm telling you to do . . ."

"Or what, Dad?" Tyler said.

He walked around the net and shook hands with Jeff and Andi. "Nice match," he said. Jeff and Andi were stunned. Was he quitting after one set? Apparently. Tyler looked over his shoulder at Terri and said, "Sorry, sis, but I'm done here. I can't do this anymore."

He dropped his racquet on his racquet bag and walked off the court. No one knew quite what was happening. Terri walked around the net and also shook hands with Jeff and Andi.

"I don't blame him," she said softly. "I'm sorry you didn't get to finish the match, but you were going to win anyway."

She walked over to her chair and plopped down in it.

"What now?" Jeff said.

"I have no idea," Andi answered. "I have no idea."

36

THE FOUR COACHES WALKED OFF TO FIND A QUIET SPOT TO talk while the players and fans waited.

Most fans didn't understand the situation. Since Tyler Porter had walked off, Merion had won the mixed doubles match: 7–6, default, in tennis terms. That meant the Mustangs had won the match 5–4 and the two schools were in a dead heat for the conference title at 11–1 and the potential tiebreaker—individual matches won—was also a tie at 9–9.

The original plan had been to hold a blind draw to see if the tiebreak set to decide who won the championship would be between the number one boys or the number one girls. Now, though, it appeared that Villanova's number one boy wasn't available.

Mr. Porter had also disappeared. Whether he had

gone after Tyler or just left, no one knew—or much cared.

After a few minutes, the crowd started to get restless. Word had passed among them that some sort of a tiebreak needed to be played. Andi, sitting with her teammates, looked up and saw Tom Michaels and a camera crew arriving along with Stevie Thomas. That had been the plan—to arrive late enough that the agents wouldn't get spooked and flee. There was a man dressed in a suit with Mr. Michaels. Andi guessed it was Tom Ross, the agent her parents were friends with.

The coaches finally returned, and the two Villanova coaches went straight to Terri Porter and began talking to her intently. Andi's guess was that they were telling her she would have to play singles against Andi to decide the conference title. She was surprised when Terri pulled out her cell phone and made a call.

Coach Foster and Coach Wentworth arrived at that moment.

"Here's what's been decided," Coach Foster said. "Since the mixed doubles match never actually finished except on the scoreboard, we've agreed that the tiebreak set will be mixed doubles . . ."

"But Tyler Porter left," Jeff said.

Coach Foster held up a hand. "Let me finish, Michaels. Terri Porter is trying to call her brother right now. All four coaches have agreed that, if he's willing to come back, we will keep his father away. It's the responsibility of the Villanova coaches, but we'll help if need be. We've also asked Joan O'Grady to help if at all possible.

"*If* he's not back here in ten minutes, they'll go with their number two boy, Harry Winslow, in his place."

"He's pretty good," Gary Morrissey said. "I can tell you that firsthand."

Everyone laughed nervously.

"Michaels, Carillo, go warm up a little. We'll start exactly nine minutes from now with or without Tyler Porter."

"We should let Terri warm up with us," Andi said.

Both coaches nodded and Coach Foster said: "Good idea."

Terri Porter was off the phone. Andi and Jeff walked over to her. "What's the deal?" they asked.

"Tyler's on his way back," she said. "He made me promise we'd both refuse to go to IMG in the fall. He also said if he saw my dad in the crowd, he'd default on the spot."

"Might be less risky if you just play with Winslow," Jeff said.

Terri smiled at Jeff. "Tyler will be fine," she said. "Plus, I like the idea of not going to IMG."

They'd been warming up for five minutes when Tyler

jogged onto the court to huge cheers from the Villanova fans—who still didn't quite know what had happened, but were happy to see him. Someone from the school had found a wireless microphone so Coach Foster could explain to everyone what was about to happen.

The four players met at the net and everyone shook hands.

"Glad to see you here, Tyler," Andi said.

"Me too," Tyler said. "I'm sorry about before."

Andi and Jeff both waved their racquets at him to say, "Forget it."

"Let's play," Jeff said.

And so they did.

Tyler was again serving flawlessly. The Porters broke Jeff in the sixth game of the set to lead 4–2, but Andi and Jeff broke Terri back in the next game and Andi then held for 4–all.

Tyler held for a third straight time and Jeff had to serve down 4–5—the entire season on the line.

He got nervous—double-faulting for 0–15, then popping in a weak second serve that Tyler crushed for a winner. They were down 0–30, two points from losing the match.

Andi stopped Jeff as he walked back to serve. "Take a deep breath," she said. "Just play tennis and you'll be fine." And then she added: "Try something a little different right now."

Jeff knew what she was telling him. Rather than try to blast his first serve, he would try to catch Terri off-balance. He hit a high-twisting serve that Terri had to hit shoulder-high from the middle of the doubles' alley. The return knuckled back and before Jeff could try to close on it, Andi poached—changed sides of the court—and slammed an untouchable volley down the middle.

"Thanks, partner," Jeff said—both for the advice and the volley.

His confidence back, he blasted a first serve down the middle that Tyler lunged at but never touched.

"Good one," she said.

"Are you sure it was good?" Jeff said, not certain.

"It was good," Terri—who had the best view of it—said. "Thirty-all."

Jeff hit two more excellent first serves and held to 5–5.

The tension was now almost unbearable.

Both girls held to 6–all.

Coach Foster stepped onto the court for a moment. "We'll now play a tiebreak game to decide the tiebreak set," he told the crowd. "First team to 7 with a two-point margin wins everything."

The way he said "wins everything" sent a shudder through Andi. She'd played big matches—won some, lost some, but never anything like this. She reminded herself that all four players were in the same boat.

Tyler started the tiebreak by serving a clean ace. For the first time all day he showed emotion that was strictly about tennis, pumping his fist and saying, "Come on now, Ty, come on!"

At 5–5, Jeff served, trying to get to match point. He hit an excellent first serve, but Tyler crushed it back, and it went right in-between Jeff and Andi. They never had a chance to touch the ball.

It was 6–5 for the Porters—and the match was on Terri's racquet, serving to Jeff, who suddenly felt as if he had a case of the shakes.

She spun her first serve, but it landed so deep in the serving box that Jeff had to go shoulder high to get his racquet to it. Fortunately, his return landed right at Tyler's feet and he had to half-volley it. Even so, it was on Jeff's side of the court and he had to charge to get it. He did and was able to pull Terri wide to get to the ball. But the shot was a balloon and she lined up a forehand and hit it right at Andi.

How Andi fought the ball off, Jeff would never know, but she punched it in-between the two Porters. Both dove for it; Tyler got his racquet on the ball but couldn't clear the net. They had survived. It was 6–all.

It went to 7–all with Andi serving to Terri. She hit a serve similar to the one that Terri had tried on match point. This time, it was Jeff who poached to hit a winner.

Now, it was Tyler's turn to serve down match point at 7–8. Jeff was playing the ad court and he guessed Tyler would go wide and take something off the serve to make sure he didn't face a second serve.

He guessed right. Even so, he practically had to lunge to get the high hopping serve back and Tyler closed on it. Jeff was certain he'd blast a forehand down the middle, but instead he cracked it in the direction of the deuce alley. Somehow, Andi hadn't been fooled. She chased the ball down as it landed in the middle of the alley, angling off the court, wound up and hit a perfect forehand down the line. The only question was whether it would land inside the sideline or outside. Jeff couldn't tell from where he was standing where the ball had landed. But he saw Tyler Porter hold his left-hand palm down—the sign that a close shot was good.

Jeff almost expected to hear Mr. Porter's voice coming from somewhere screaming, "It was out!" Instead, he heard Andi screaming and running to hug him. Out of the corner of one eye, Jeff saw the twins hugging each other and sensed they were crying on each other's shoulders.

He and Andi walked to the net and waited for them. All four had tears in their eyes as they shook hands.

"Never enjoyed a match more than that one," Tyler said as they all leaned across the net to exchange hugs.

"Me neither," Andi said.

Around them, everyone was clapping and cheering—for both teams. It was, Andi thought later, proof of how great tennis could be when everyone just played tennis.

Now, though, the fun part of the day was over.

37

ANDI'S AND JEFF'S PARENTS WERE BOTH WAITING TO congratulate them once they had finished shaking hands with everyone from Villanova. Mark Appleman, who was apparently the principal at Bryn Mawr Tech and the executive director of the suburban Philadelphia middle school sports conference, magically appeared with a large trophy.

He was handed the wireless microphone and asked that Merion's coaches come forward to accept the trophy. Andi noticed the coaches waving in their direction and pointing in the direction of Mr. Appleman.

"*You* go get it," Coach Foster said. "You and Jeff."

She and Jeff worked their way to Mr. Appleman, who appeared confused at first, but quickly recovered. He put his hand over the microphone, leaned over and said, "I'm going to introduce you two as team captains."

That was fine with Jeff and Andi even though no one had ever actually been named a captain.

"It's my pleasure," he said, microphone again open, "to present the championship trophy for 2021 to Merion's captains, Andrea Carillo and Jeff Michaels! Congratulations!"

He handed the trophy to the two of them to hold up together—which they did.

"One of you should say a couple of words," he said.

"You do it," Jeff said.

"Why me?" Andi said.

"How many singles matches did you lose?"

She knew when she was beaten. She reluctantly accepted the microphone handed to her by Mr. Appleman.

"On behalf of Jeff and myself, I'd first like to congratulate and thank everyone from Villanova. You guys were great competitors and great sportsmen. It was a pleasure to compete with you."

She paused for everyone to applaud. The Villanova players all waved in her direction.

"And, on behalf of Jeff and myself, I'd like to thank all of our teammates and our coaches. Jeff and I won the last point today, but it took every single one of us to win this trophy." She nodded at Jeff, who held the trophy aloft again.

"Last, but far from least, I'd like to thank everyone

who came out today to support both teams. It was so much fun to play in front of all of you. Here's to defending our title next year!"

She handed the mike back to Mr. Appleman and gave Jeff another hug—an awkward one since he was still holding the trophy. Then they took a team picture with all ten players and the two coaches.

As Andi started to walk back to her parents, she heard a voice say behind her. "Season's over. You ready to talk now?"

It was—no surprise—Renee Stubing, the most confident of the agents. Andi saw Stevie Thomas and Jeff's dad walking in her direction.

"I think you need to talk to these guys, not me," she said.

For once, Renee Stubing was caught off guard. "What are you talking about?"

Stevie was holding up a contract—Andi wasn't even sure which one.

"This," he said. "The contract you offered an eleven-year-old girl a couple of days ago."

Stubing's eyes narrowed, and she shot Andi a look of clear disgust.

"There's nothing illegal or against the rules in that contract," she said, recovering quickly. "What would there be for me to say?"

"I don't know, Renee," Tom Michaels said. "Maybe

the fact that you're basically promising to launder money through Andi's parents to Andi in an attempt to make her a professional without her having to declare herself as a professional."

Stubing laughed. "Common practice," she said. "Go talk to the Porters about their deal with Aces."

"We already did," Stevie said. "We've got a copy of their contract, too. And now we've got you on the record admitting that you do this all the time."

"I wasn't on the record," Stubing said. "There's no camera."

Tom Michaels laughed. "You think only a camera means you're on the record, Ms. Stubing? Come on, you're smarter than that."

Andi noticed that Joan O'Grady and a man she guessed was Gary Morrissey's dad were now standing behind Stevie and Mr. Michaels spectating. Tad Walters and Monica Alston were both there, too. Jeff, who had walked up behind Andi, pointed at them, and Stevie and Mr. Michaels turned around.

Stevie grinned. "Aha, the other non-agents have arrived. We've got your contracts for Andi and her parents, too—anyone care to comment, on camera or off?"

They all looked terrified. It was Tad Walters who finally said something. Pointing a finger at Andi he said, "You tricked us, you little . . ." He stopped when Alston grabbed his arm, apparently digging her nails into it because instead of finishing the sentence he yelped in pain.

Tom Michaels was talking again. "We don't need any of you on camera. We've already taped an interview with Tom Ross, who has been in your business for almost forty years, explaining how this works and how it's worked for years. We're about to interview the Porter twins, who are happy to talk about the deal their dad made with you, Mr. Morrissey. But, if you'd like to tell your side, we're happy to listen."

"You've already made up your minds," Stubing said. "You've already judged us guilty."

"We're not the judges," Stevie said. "We report. The public judges."

Jeff was suddenly reminded of the old TV show *Dragnet* that he had watched with his parents in the past.

"Just the facts, ma'am," he said, trying to keep a straight face. "All we want are the facts."

Their jobs for the day done, Jeff and Andi went off to take much-needed showers. After lingering to celebrate for a while with their teammates, they headed back to the courts, which were now almost empty, to the spot where Tom Michaels and his crew had set up.

All of the agents were gone except for Alston,

who was standing in front of the camera along with Mr. Michaels. Stevie stood to the side, cell phone recorder in his hand.

"So, you think this sort of thing is defensible then? Recruiting an eleven-year-old girl *and* subverting the rules by paying her through her parents?"

Alston forced a smile. "It's a win-win. The child comes into a lot of money at some point and some of it is guaranteed from the start."

"What percentage would you say is guaranteed?" Tom Michaels said.

"It depends on how much they win," Alston answered.

"Interesting you use the term 'child,'" he said. "That's certainly accurate. Last question: how many girls would you say have signed contracts around the country before the age of fourteen in the last twenty years?"

Alston smiled as if she'd been handed a hanging curveball. "Around the country?" she said. "Into the hundreds."

"And how many of those hundreds have gone on to successful careers in tennis?"

The smile faded from Alston's face. "Well, um, I don't have, you know, exact numbers."

"I can think of Coco Gauff," Tom Michaels said. "Can you give me any other names?"

For a moment Alston didn't answer. Mr. Michaels simply left the microphone in front of her. "I'm sure there are others," she finally said. "I just don't have their names in front of me."

Tom Michaels smiled and gave his cameraman a wrap sign.

"Thank you, Ms. Alston," he said, but Alston was already gone, stalking past Stevie, who was waiting to ask her follow-ups. Tad Walters was waiting and they practically fled, leaving everyone else watching them depart, smiles on their faces.

"We got 'em all," Stevie said. "We made sure none of them could hear Tom's questions so they wouldn't have time to prep some cooked-up non-answer. There are going to be a lot of unhappy agents around the country come Saturday night."

The plan was for Stevie's story to go up online at 10 p.m.—the same time that the NBC Sports–Philadelphia story would air.

Andi's parents introduced Andi and Jeff to Tom Ross.

"What effect do you think this will have on the agent business?" Andi asked him as they shook hands.

Ross smiled. "Nothing changes what agents do," he said. "Unless someone makes a rule saying that parents can't sign contracts of any kind for their kids until they're at least sixteen—I'd even say eighteen would be better—they'll keep doing what they do. I promise you, there are a lot more Bart Porters out there than Tony Carillos."

"How did Tyler and Terri do talking to you?" Jeff asked.

"They did great," Mr. Michaels said. "But I don't envy them what comes next—whatever it is."

"It's so unfair, that having talent can be such a burden to kids," Andi said. She turned to her parents. "I'm so grateful to have you as my parents."

"A-men to that," Jeff said.

"Well, even though my daughter isn't going to make me rich, I think this calls for a celebration," Tony Carillo said. "Anybody up for a Del Frisco's steak?"

"Do you think we can get a table this late?" Andi's mom asked.

"I'll check," Tom Michaels said, taking out his phone.

"Feel like tennis tomorrow?" Andi asked Jeff as they left the adults to work out the celebration details.

"Sure," Jeff said, happy to carry on their usual Saturday arrangement. "And then some pizza?"

"Actually, I was thinking we might skip the food court and go to a movie instead. You know, try something new."

She looked at Jeff with an intense expression.

For a split second, Jeff didn't get it. Then he did.

"Hot dog, popcorn, and a movie," he finally answered with a huge smile. "Sounds perfect to me."

"A-men to that," Andi said. "A-men to that."